WENATCHEE BEND

WENATCHEE BEND

by

Giff Cheshire

The Golden West Large Print Books
Long Preston, North Yorkshire,
BD23 4ND, England.

British Library Cataloguing in Publication Data.

Cheshire, Giff
 Wenatchee bend.

 A catalogue record of this book is
 available from the British Library

 ISBN   978-1-84262-920-8 pbk

Cover illustration © Michael Thomas

The moral right of the author has been asserted

Published in Large Print 2012 by arrangement with
Golden West Literary Agency

The Golden West Large Print is an imprint of Library Magna
Books Ltd.

Printed and bound in Great Britain by
T.J. (International) Ltd., Cornwall, PL28 8RW

CHAPTER ONE

The wind from Canada seemed bent on flattening everything standing in the valley and freezing the rest, although winter was still weeks away. Since noon Twig Tully had watched it grow from quiet gusts to a shrieking and steady force. By midafternoon it had threatened to sweep up herd, horses, and riders and deposit them farther south than they could travel in the weeks of trailing still ahead. And that, Twig had thought, would at least be a solution to his problem.

The wind hadn't got that strong, although the supper fire smoke boiled off at ground level and scattered embers into the rocks, sagebrush, and the trees along the river. But the cold had deepened until the heat of the fire seemed hardly to reach the kettle and coffeepot swinging on the rod above. Even less got to the punchers who sat on their heels with Twig. All of them held out unfeeling hands in hope of getting them thawed enough eat the first hot meal since daybreak.

Two of the men were silent and gloomy, knowing that the warmth they managed to soak up would be blown away again when they rode out, presently, to relieve the cocktail guard. Another, hunkered next to Twig, could think further ahead than that. 'What you going to do in the morning?' he asked. 'Toss a coin or make a guess?'

'Dunno.' Twig tried to force a grin onto his pinched mouth. 'I reckon one's about as good as the other.'

They all looked at him then, and in varying degrees of sympathy. They had more leeway in their simple riding jobs, more right to be themselves, than he would ever be given, and they knew it. They understood that his problem wasn't merely what to do in this unseasonal bad weather that had caught them with a herd far out on the homebound trail. He had to figure out what Oak Tully, his father, would do about it if Oak were there.

It wasn't only that, being crippled badly now for many years, Oak watched things like OT was a chessboard resting on the arms of his wheelchair and his opponent all the things that could go wrong on a cattle operation that reached out over hundreds of miles. During the three years he had run the trail end of the operation, Twig reflected, he had built up to the place where every decision was a thing of dread, a point where he went on trial with the odds not in his favor. For even longer this sense of being tried and found wanting had been bait to a rebellious, stubborn streak in him that increased the odds against him.

And in the morning there would be another decision to be made—

'Hey, Twig!'

Although the call was directed at the trail boss, all the men at the fire turned their heads to look. A puncher walking in from the horse band pointed with his hand but waited until he got closer to yell again.

'Here comes the pickup crew from Injun Creek. Looks to me like your wet nurse is along.'

'Dill?' Johnny Danbo said at Twig's elbow. 'Who dealt him in on this?'

'When that jigger smells trouble for Twig,' Buck Shipley answered, 'he don't wait to be dealt in.'

Twig agreed and let his gaze slide across the flat where the Okanogan blended its water with that of the Columbia. The lights of Brown's Landing twinkled in the far distance on the Columbia's downstream shore. Upwind from his line of sight the new OT steers were trying to feed on bunchgrass already crisp with ice. He located the Injun Creek riders off to the left of the cattle. They came from the direction of the little river town, where they had probably stopped to warm their insides. Even so, they were all three hunched in the saddle, and Twig knew why they were still miserable. To get over from the Injun Creek side, they had had to swim the Columbia, which was the largest river in the Northwest.

His study settled reluctantly on the largest of the men, a hard and arrogant shape even in the fading light. His faint hope of some escape expired. It was Dill Humminger. As the OT range boss Dill still held down the biggest job on the biggest spread in the Wenatchee Bend, but he would never forget that once he had been Oak's sole lieutenant. There was something more he was even less apt to forget. Oak having been kept out of a saddle so long, it had fallen to Dill to give the son and heir his training in the business. A training that in Dill's eyes wasn't and would never be finished.

Dill's arrival left Twig with little time to solve the problem that had troubled him all afternoon. There were seven hundred winter feeders in the herd, which he had bought for OT from outfits scattered along the Okanogan. Oak himself had given the orders as to their disposition: a hundred head to Injun Creek, six hundred to the hay ranch on the Peshastin. Oak would expect this to be done to the exact head except for good cause. Come good cause, he would expect his orders to be changed.

So the latest in a long line of decision-trials was whether this sudden threat of foul weather was cause or wasn't. If it was, the thing to do was to swim the whole herd over the Columbia and hustle it to Injun Creek, only a day's trailing distant. The west-side trail was a tough one and a week long in the best weather. And even Oak Tully wasn't rich enough to gamble twenty thousand in beef cattle on it.

It was Twig's private opinion that the freezing wind was a backlash of a polar storm hundreds of miles north that might die as quickly as it had arrived. He had never known of a blizzard, with snow and ice and all their attendance dangers, to arrive in the middle of November. Yet, according to the old-timers, it had happened.

Twig still hung on the horns of uncertainty when the pickup crew reached the camp. They were wet to the waist from the swim and numbed speechless. Dill gave Twig no more than a nod and a grunt and moved stiffly to the fire. His men were on his heels and as surly as Dill seemed. Twig's trail hands didn't like them any better than he did, but they knew misery when they saw it. They took charge of the horses, and one of them began to pour hot coffee from the swinging black pot.

Dill didn't give Twig his attention until he had thawed a little and swallowed a lot of coffee. A part of his condescension came from having put in twelve more years of life than Twig's own twenty-three. Part resulted from about the same difference in their

11

experience. But mostly it came from his feeling that the younger man had never and would never measure up to the role to which he had by mischance been born.

He said in a voice of deceitful mildness, 'They told me at the landing you got here two-three hours before dark.'

'That's right,' Twig agreed, smelling a trap and trying to edge off from it.

'So you had plenty of time to swim the critters before you made camp. Too bad you didn't.'

The contrary streak that so often worked against Twig moved right up front with that. He said with a patience he didn't feel, 'They caught hell all afternoon and were too beat to throw into the water on a day like this.'

'What kind of day do you think tomorrow'll be?'

'Better,' Twig said flatly. 'This wind's a freak.'

'And you bet six hundred beef steers on that.'

'Six hundred? Injun Creek's only to get–'

'I know what Injun Creek's to get. You should've crossed the whole kaboodle and run for cover. Since you didn't this afternoon, you better in the morning.'

Dill was putting it in the form of condescending advice, for he no longer had authority over cattle that wasn't loose on one of the numerous ranges. Twig looked at him bleakly, knowing that he had been foxed and boxed. No point now in saying he'd meant to see how it looked in the morning before he went so far as to divert the whole trail herd. Dill had got in his criticism and opinion the first rattle out of the box. The only way to avoid following it, and looking like he'd had to be corrected by an older and wiser man, was to commit himself immediately to the opposite course.

Which was exactly what Dill wanted him to do.

The others at the fire had started to eat and then had stopped to listen. Twig's men were watching him with special interest. They knew as well as he did Dill expected a long siege of bad weather and was trying to manipulate Twig so he would wind up with his tail caught in the wringer. Twig knew they wanted him to defy the man and his wiliness and beat him.

Twig was ready to shove in his stack, but Dill didn't give him the chance just then. Walking over to the fire, the range boss began to fill a plate with stew. He didn't want to seem to be pushing too hard.

Two of the trail hands rode out to relieve the men on guard. Dried out and fed, Dill and his Indian Creekers rode back to the landing, preferring to do any further warming up there in the saloon. Twig offered the same privilege to the trail hands loitering

13

around the campfire, but they declined. They had all ridden for OT for years. Once they were alone, Pink Ashley looked at Twig with eyes that showed both distaste and amusement.

'That long-coupled galoot,' he drawled. 'If he wasn't convinced we're in for a heller, he wouldn't have gone on record with all that free advice. He'd look bad to Oak himself if you took it and it turned mild as lambin' weather.'

'He's convinced,' Twig agreed.

'Maybe it's his corns,' Ferd Darling said with a grin. 'Another edge he's got from bein' so much older than you are.'

But they weren't trying to tell him what to do. It was something they wanted him to decide, and whichever way it was they would go along.

Twig went to sleep still puzzled and uneasy. And then came relief. When he rolled out of his blankets to stand the last guard with Johnny Danbo, he found that the wind had slacked off. There was a noticeable rise in temperature. It seemed to let him out of his dilemma simply by removing it.

The air was even warmer when he and Danbo rode back to a camp aroused for the new day's work. The smoke of the fire rose almost straight up by then. Twig saw his relief reflected on the faces of his men. There was a contrasting moodiness in Dill's eyes.

14

Then the light strengthened to show, low on the northern skyline, a narrow band of black clouds. Twig didn't know what to make of them. They could mean that the polar storm had come closer, with the turbulence on its edge moved farther south. Yet there wasn't wind enough to drive the clouds this way very fast.

That left the weather prospects on balance and the way open to avoid taking Dill's tricky advice without flying in the face of common sense to defy him. The season was too early for bad weather of any size. And the Peshastin allotment would be a hundred miles from where Oak planned to winter it if it went to Injun Creek on the basis of a false alarm.

Right after breakfast he settled it, saying calmly 'Well, let's cut the Injun Creek allotment. We got a long trail ahead of us with the rest.'

'Well, I warned you,' Dill said.

'That's right,' Twig agreed. 'You did.'

The cutting began immediately and would take a while. Once it was going, Twig turned his horse west. He reached the stage and freight road just as the morning stage rattled past, heading for the mining camps at Conconully and Ruby, up in the country where he had bought the cattle. At the far edge of the valley where there was flat benchland, lay low buttes covered with sage and exposed rock. Beyond them snow-peaked mountains rose against what in that direction was an untroubled sky.

Twig turned the horse south toward the river port Judah Brown had founded to serve as a transfer point between the down-country and the inland mines and cattle ranges. Presently he saw a dozen or so raw-lumber buildings ahead of him. Brown House stood on one side of the rutted road, Brown's Mercantile on the other, and a wharf boat bobbed at the end of the street. A pack string down there was loading for the interior, and beyond the floating warehouse rose the stack, staffs, and pilothouse of either the *Chief* or the *Arrow,* which also were Brown properties. A saloon, blacksmith shop, and a handful of unpainted houses made up the rest of the town.

Twig had tied his reins to the pole below the store porch when he looked up to see somebody he hadn't expected to see there. She was also a Brown appendage, Melissa by name. But she handled the freight and passenger business of the river line on the Wenatchee City end. And that was sixty miles downstream.

She hadn't noticed him, for she was reading something that seemed to have come up in the mail. She had a scarf wrapped around her head and throat, with a buffalo coat draped on her shoulders. Twig wondered what she was dong up here, for the Brown family didn't incline toward taking things easy. The sons, Abner and Zeke, ran the two steamers that on alternate days came up a reach of river few pilots cared to tackle.

All at once Melissa looked up and saw him, and her expression conveyed no great pleasure on her part at the unlikely encounter. She was a slender, fair girl. Even a man who had come not to like her any better than she had come not to like him had to admit she was extremely pretty.

'Well,' Twig said, ducking under the rail, stepping onto the porch and touching his hat. 'Howdy, Melissa. What're you doing so far from home?'

'Visiting my own father's away from home?'

She was going to be testy again, for she knew what he meant. She still lived in Wenatchee City and had grown up there. He had known her nearly all his life, and they had been good friends until another young woman came to live there whom Melissa had detested on sight.

'Man, you get sweeter every time we see each other,' Twig said.

'And it seems to me you get more stupid.' But Melissa smiled finally. 'I don't have to ask what you're dong up here. How was the buying trip?'

'So you know I went on a buying trip.'

'What goes on in the Wenatchee everybody doesn't hear about?'

'I don't know. Oak don't let me hang around there much, anymore.'

'You better do something about that,' Melissa said. 'Dill Humminger's cutting in on your girl.'

Twig frowned, although that wasn't news to him. 'You know Lorna Milne isn't my girl.'

'But you wish she was, and you're sure losing ground. Dill had her to the lodge dance last week while you were up there in the Okanogan looking at cattle.'

Twig knew Melissa was roweling rather than telling him something to help him. The only thing she liked less than his interest in Lorna was Lorna herself. But that wasn't the only place she had come to find nearly as much fault with him as Oak found. Another place was Oak, himself, for she said he let himself be treated as if he was only a mindless extension of his father. Which hadn't been telling him anything newer than what she had just said about Lorna and Dill.

'Well, don't hold your breath waiting,' Twig said stiffly, 'for me to bust out in tears.'

'That's not what I'm waiting for,' Melissa said with a strange smile.

She turned abruptly and without farewell stepped down to the road. He couldn't help watching after her, wondering what she had

18

meant by that. She was nearly across the road when a gust of wind came from somewhere and hit her hard enough to turn her half around. He hardly felt it on the porch, and his mouth dropped open at its suddenness and force. Melissa ran on across and disappeared into the hotel without looking his way again.

Twig hurried over to the store door. A thermometer-barometer set hung by the door, nailed there by Judah Brown as a public service. Twig made a puzzling study of both instruments. The temperature hung at freezing, colder than it had been when he came off night guard. The atmospheric pressure was low enough to threaten colder weather yet and explained the gust of wind out of the deceptive calm of the morning. Twig's mouth dropped open. It also explained what Dill had tried to pass off as an accurate weather nose. Dill had seen this thing and its warning before he even arrived at the trail camp. He had kept it to himself, which he wouldn't have done if he hadn't been digging a pit.

Twig saw through the door glass that Judah Brown was watching him with moody eyes. There were no customers, and Judah was warming his broad backside at the stove while he worked on a cigar. Twig had meant to put in an order for supplies to be picked up when the Peshastin herd came by. His disturbing thoughts about bringing it this way after the warning turned him away from the door.

Yet the thought of going back to the herd and reversing himself was intolerable. A barometer could only hint at what might happen weatherwise within the next day or two. It certainly was no more infallible than the corns Ferd Darling had attributed to Dill the night before.

For a moment Twig was tempted to turn once again and ask Judah what he thought, for Judah had lived in this country now for several years. Yet he was afraid to. If Judah supported Dill's conclusions from the barometer reading he would have to give in and follow Dill's advice. But if he didn't follow it and lost the Peshastins or a costly part of them, he'd still be doing what Dill really wanted. The only self-respecting course and one with which even Melissa Brown could find no fault, would be not to worry so much about what Oak would think, defy Dill, and still keep his tail out of the crack of the door.

The Injun Creek cut was to be swum at the mouth of the Okanogan. So Twig turned his horse up the sandy shore of the Columbia, which at that point ran west. He had barely left the landing when another stiff gust of wind made him grab his hat. It lifted trash from the ground and sent it scurrying. This gust was colder, but it only made Twig set his jaw.

He reached the night's bed ground to find that the men had finished cutting. The Peshastin steers stood off to the west, his own men holding them and waiting for his order to trail. Twig rose in the stirrup, caught somebody's attention, and waved them west into whatever awaited them. Then he slanted over to where Dill sat his horse, waiting with the two Injun Creek punchers and a much smaller bunch of cattle.

Until it was over the river and on the Injun Creek side, even this cut was in the trail boss's charge, and Dill's presence made no difference. Ignoring Dill, Twig waved a hand at the punchers. 'What're you sittin' there for? Come on. Let's get 'em over the river.'

Dill flung him a look of annoyance, not liking interference half as well as he liked to interfere. His punchers looked startled but obeyed the order and began to work the cut into motion.

CHAPTER TWO

It was nearly noon when Twig tied his horse again in front of the store at Brown's Landing. He was wet to the skin and half paralyzed but that was nothing compared to the cold dread that had taken possession of him. He had had his triumph over Dill by taking charge of the river swim, but it had been short lasting.

The swim had been a mean one. The steers had balked at going into the water at all and had practically to be picked up and thrown in. It proved how right Dill had been when he said they, and even the whole herd, should have been crossed the day before. It had been nip and tuck for both men and animals to reach the far side. By the time they were over the gusts had turned into a steady freezing wind. The inky clouds that had been only a stripe on the horizon at dawn now covered half the sky.

But there had been no changing it by then, Twig knew, even if he could have bowed his neck to do so.

Now he had to pick up the supplies he hadn't even ordered. But waiting would let him dry out a bit before he set out in the freezing blast to catch up with his own men. He loosened his saddlebags and carried them into the store. Judah Brown was still basking in the heat of the big stove. He had lighted a fresh cigar. Midday was his slack period, the morning's stage and steamer departed, the afternoon arrivals not yet in. Shaking in cold misery, Twig joined him wordlessly.

Judah wasn't wordless. He took the cigar from his lips and said, 'You look a mite blue.' He went behind the counter, lifted a jug from underneath, and splashed a tin cup half full of whisky, which he brought back and held out. 'You better down this. It ain't going to be any warmer where you're headin'.'

'Th–thanks.' Twig's teeth had started clicking like a telegraph key. 'Wh–what do you think it's gonna do, J–Judah.'

Judah shrugged his thick shoulders. 'Only fools and tenderfeet try to call the turn in this country. On both weather and women.' So he must have observed the less than cordial exchange with Melissa on the porch that morning. 'How's your dad?'

'Same as always,' Twig said.

Judah knew pretty well how that would be. He had run a store in Wenatchee City before he decided to build his own metropolis up here in the lonely sagebrush. He and Oak were well acquainted, even if something less than friends.

'Good,' Judah said. 'If you've got an order, I better be puttin' it up while you're melting off the frost.'

'Yeah.' Twig had finished the whisky, and it had taken the twitches out of his jaw. 'A couple of sides of bacon and a bag of coffee. Some flour and salt. A few bags of Bull and some matches.'

Judah wrote it down in the order book he had taken from his apron pocket. He said around the cigar, 'Melissa was tellin' me you've got the same name as your dad, which is why they call you Twig. I always wondered why they did.'

'Better than Junior,' Twig said. He was surprised that Melissa ever discussed him, although he remembered telling her once what his real name was. 'But not much.'

Judah nodded. 'I guess it keeps you feelin' kind of shrunk.'

Twig had thought himself to be the only one with that insight. The nickname had never bothered him when he was a boy, but the older he got the more it kept him reminded that he was only an appendage of Oak. An acorn that had sprouted in Oak's shadow and never grew much because it was shut off from the sun itself. He had wondered many times how it would feel to have roots of his own and the ability to throw his own shadow.

Judah went off to fill the order. Twig's clothes had begun to steam. He moved back from the stove, wondering what had made Judah mention the nickname. That was a pretty personal subject for idle talk.

It didn't take long to put up the supplies. When he was through, Judah picked up his cigar, relighted it thoughtfully, and came back.

He had a hesitant look when he said, 'I guess Oak thinks pretty well of Humminger.'

'Sure,' Twig agreed. 'Dill started to work for him when he was half grown, and he never rode for anybody else.'

'How do you feel about him?'

'Well–' Twig cut him a look of inquiry. This made two Browns who had brought up the subject of Dill that day. 'I don't guess it's any secret that we don't hit it off.'

'Then maybe it ain't out of line to give you a nudge that would have no effect on Oak. At least if it come from me.'

'Nudge? What about?'

Judah answered obliquely. 'Well, has Humminger got authority to sell OT cattle? I mean, make the deals, write bills of sale, collect?'

'He used to have,' Twig said. 'It had to be that way after Oak got hurt and couldn't get around very good himself.'

'Humminger still got it?' Judah pressed.

'I – don't know.' Twig wasn't brushing aside the strangely personal question. He really didn't know. For a number of years Dill had been Oak's sole agent in about everything having to do with the ranch's business with outsiders. Now that the job had been split in two, Twig himself handled some of it, although he had never been given anything resembling a power of attorney. 'I suppose he has.'

That gave Judah some kind of satisfaction that made him nod to himself, like a man who had filled a poker hand. 'Who handles the books?' he asked.

'Oak takes care of the ranch books. Dill and the foremen handle the bookkeeping for the ranges. That's the way it works on most spreads.'

'Yeah.' Judah nodded gravely, but again to himself. 'That's how I figured it.'

'What are you trying to say?'

'Never said I'd say anything – only that I'd give you a nudge.'

And nudge it had been. Twig regarded the cherry-red side of the stove with puzzled eyes. It was evident that Judah didn't like Dill, who was inclined to think he threw a shadow nearly as long as Oak's in his manner toward the people of the country. Judah knew or had guessed something and figured that a word to the wise was sufficient. Well, maybe it was. Dill had a free

26

hand with OT's ranges and a boss who couldn't get around very much to see things first hand. Would he cheat on Oak, the man to whom he had given his whole working life? If he would, he had more reason than jealousy for not wanting Oak's son in a position where he could do the checking up.

Twig wasn't completely dried out, but he was in a hurry to catch up with the Peshastin drive. The store bill wasn't large, so he paid it out of pocket, although the ranch had charge accounts all over the country. He shook hands with Judah, carried out the bulging saddlebags, and was soon on his way down the river.

He was following a historic trail that for about ten years had been one of the big cattle trails of the West, this one leading to the rich mines of the Cariboo deep in Canada. The trail and the highly profitable business it opened had given Oak his start, and that was when Dill first went to work for him. It was on one of the last drives that Oak got hurt and crippled for life.

Twig didn't like Dill a little bit but in view of that background he hated to believe what he was thinking. Yet Judah wasn't a man to throw suspicion on him without being very sure of himself. Brown's Landing was the focal point of this end of the country and of much of the country on the opposite side of the river. Sooner or later Judah heard a little or a lot about everything that went on within many miles of him.

Twig was hardly a mile away from the landing when he had to let the matter drop and think again of the weather. Without his noticing at first, a wispy snow had started to sift down. When he looked up with startled eyes it was to see a sky black every way he looked. In another ten minutes the first floury snow had turned into fat, dry flakes that filled a steady wind and stuck where they fell. The cold was taking on a really cutting edge, and the only question remaining was whether this would be of short life or lasting.

He caught up with the Peshastins somewhere north of the Methow River, although by then he could only guess where they were. The storm had proved it was in dead earnest, and defining landmarks had been masked out. The steers had trailed out of the mouth of the Okanogan Valley, so the wind wasn't quite so strong. But the air was intensely cold, the snow fell heavily. He found the cattle bunched up and steaming, with the riders having trouble keeping them moving at all.

Ashley and Darling were on drag and when Twig drew in behind them and yelled they stopped their horses. They said the horse band had been put ahead to give the steers something to follow, and Shipley was riding point. Rankin and Danbo had their hands more than full on the flanks, trying to keep bobbers from disappearing into the trailside brush. The drag riders could only hammer away with their rope ends and cuss.

Twig didn't try to blame it on anything but his own bullheadedness. He told them how he had seen the barometer that had convinced Dill this was coming. He'd gone ahead, anyway and thrown five good men and a small fortune in beef into the very teeth of it. There was no chance of getting the steers to swim the river without considerable improvement in the weather, but they could turn back and find a place where there was more feed available.

'Turn back?' The punchers stared at him. Then Darling, added, 'They ain't my cattle, and it ain't my job but I'm one of them five men. And I'd risk my life for a chance to rub Dill's nose in it.' Ashley grinned and nodded his head.

That was a mixture of faith and bravado, but it made Twig feel better. 'What're we waitin' here for?' he said. 'Let's push them steers.'

It soon looked like he had only compounded his folly, for by midafternoon two inches of snow lay on the ground. By late day there were four inches, with no letup in sight. The punchers pounded the drive past the Methow, but as night neared, bare, rolling hills began to crowd against the river. This pinched the trail until the flankers had to fall back and let the steers string out even worse than before. The cattle didn't like it. They didn't like the snow that now froze to a crusty pack under their feet as fast as it fell. They bawled and balked, and every one of them figured he could do better for himself than the drivers were doing.

'We'll have a bitch of a time holdin' 'em tonight,' Shipley mused. 'And it'll be hell on us tryin' to ride herd.'

Twig was giving thought to that himself, although keeping the cattle from drifting was no more of a problem than feeding them, for by then every blade of grass was buried under freezing snow. Yet he thought he might have an answer to both problems for that one night. A mile or so ahead of them there was a point of land that crowded the trail almost to the edge of the water. If they shoved the herd past, then made their camp in the narrows, their fire would thwart the cattle's natural disposition to turn back on the trail. He had remembered a homesteader, a little farther on, who might be persuaded to sell enough hay for a slim feeding. He told the men what he was going to do and rode ahead of the drive.

The pass notched into the rocky end of the

point was slippery, but he got through and thought the steers could make it. A pocket meadow of some size lay on the leeward side of the formation. The homesteader's shack was in it somewhere but with visibility at nearly zero would be hard to find. Even the trail proved to be so, for on the flat ground south of the point it wasn't marked by banks. Twig let his horse use its own judgment until finally he heard the not too distant barking of dogs. This was a racket usually hated by cattle drivers for it made cattle nervous. But it was welcome to Twig that evening, and he turned the horse toward the noise.

The first sign of habitation was even more welcome, a big stack of hay cut from the meadow. He could make out beyond that a ramshackle barn and a couple of flimsy sheds. The barking had stopped, indicating that somebody had shut up the dogs. A moment later Twig could see the shack, too. Two dogs, trembling but grown quiet, stood below the steps, watching him with hating eyes. A man had placed himself in the doorway above them, and his eyes didn't look much friendlier. He didn't even part with a nod of the head when Twig pulled up at the bottom of the steps.

Twig had been past the place at a distance a number of times without meeting the settler, and he didn't know his name. The homesteader finally nodded, warily. He was a wedge-shaped man with shaggy hair and a flowing beard. A thin woman peered past him, and ragged small-fry looked around his legs. They didn't get much company, and Twig realized that they were only leery of what the storm had blown in.

'I've got a herd comin',' Twig said, hoping to reassure them. 'I aim to hold it in the pocket tonight.'

The settler wasn't ready to thaw out and said promptly, 'Not on my claim, you don't.'

'It's a pretty big pocket. Surely you don't claim all of it.'

'Nope, but there's no fences, and I got a haystack.'

'I know, and I'd like to buy it.'

'Not that hay.' The shaggy head shook itself adamantly. 'I got my own critters to think about.'

'Don't you have hay in the barn?'

'Not enough to winter, the way it's startin' out.'

A greedy glitter had begun to show in the man's eyes, convincing Twig that he had hay to spare and was only getting himself set to drive a hard bargain. That was something Twig didn't like about many of the dirt-farming breed beginning to clutter the country. A stockman would have done his best to help anybody's cattle in distress, and for only a fair consideration if any at all.

He had cattle-buying money left over in his belt but didn't want to be robbed of it if he could help. He quit trying to persuade and said flatly, 'Come off it. You've got hay in the barn for your team of horses and your one or two milk cows. You put up the hay in the stack to sell to somebody caught in a fix. That right?'

'You're talkin'.'

'What do you figure to get for it?'

'What you'll have to pay to get it.'

'I'll pay a fair price, and I'd set that at fifty dollars.'

'I guess your critters ain't very hungry.'

'All right. Seventy-five.'

'I gotta close this door, mister. The house is gettin' cold, and we got young 'uns.'

'A hundred.' The door started to shut and, giving in, Twig yelled, 'Then name your price!'

'Double it.'

'Two hundred? Man, I'm glad I'm not one of your critters with the heart you've got for animals.'

The settler's lip curled. 'Know where you're gonna do any better around here?'

Twig knew that was a question no amount of temper could answer in his favor. He shrugged a weary assent and paying the man put a big hole in the gold in his belt. The settler fairly grabbed it, then slammed the door, and Twig rode back to meet the cattle.

The steers made trouble, but the riders hazed them over the point and along the trail Twig had broken. By the time they left the cattle at the haystack the last light had faded from the stormy air. The settler had called his dogs indoors, Twig saw in relief, and stayed there himself. The men rode back to the point and found a place on the lee side for their camp. Not knowing of the extortion Twig had been forced to submit to, the men grew cheerful. The night promised to make the day look warm by comparison, and they wouldn't have to ride night herd. The fire would keep the cattle from turning back, and the hay would offset any inclination to drift toward any other point of the compass.

Even in their blankets it was a miserable night, for the temperature dropped to depths beyond what they had expected. Just before dawn the snowfall stopped, but the first light showed a blanket a foot deep on the levels. In the wind outside their sheltered area there were drifts much deeper. This would make for killingly slow going. It would stop them completely if the temperature rose to the melting range during the day and dropped below at night. The cattle had made short shift of the hay, which had strengthened them temporarily. But Twig didn't have much hope of other haystacks waiting down the trail, even if he could pay the prices that would be exacted for them.

All that day and through the two that followed the herd bucked its way down the pitching, winding, snow-choked trail between the hugging hills and the river. The first night there was no feed to be bought or uncovered from under the snow. It was the same the following night, although he was able to turn the cattle out of the wind and into the protection of a coulee. On the third night he paid another settler a hundred dollars for the privilege of turning the cattle into a small field of corn fodder. And then they came to Quibble Mountain, and the last of his luck ran out.

At that point the trail rose high above the river to cross a headland that fell in a long, sharp drop below the trail. Twig rode ahead to look it over and turned sick at his stomach, for the entire stretch was buried under forbidding drifts. To worsen matters, the wind was so fierce it lifted snow and drove it like a sandstorm against the rearing rocks. He didn't think anything could even live up there, let alone travel. The best he could do that night was to move the herd into the shelter of a gulch on the near side of the mountain. He didn't have much time to get over, for there was no chance of feed there for the cattle and the horses.

The riders made camp in a position that once more would hold the cattle automatically. While Danbo and Shipley started to cook the night meal, Twig rode back to the headland with the other punchers, making use of the last light. The wind had died a little and he hoped he could see well enough to tell if there was a chance of breaking a trail across the head firm and stable enough to hold up the cattle.

He found that he could see almost too well, for everything he looked at was discouraging. The snow on the bald, steep mountain held there partly because it had been plastered there by the wind. With the air calmer, he realized that almost any kind of jarring could start a slide. He didn't know with what surer aim he could have rammed his way into a cul-de-sac of disastrous proportions. They couldn't go forward, and there was no turning back, for the cattle had consumed all the feed to be had behind them.

Hunched in the saddle like a frozen letter S. Con Rankin regarded the scene with solemn eyes. 'You reckon there's any chance,' he asked, 'of getting over that thing farther back from the river?'

Twig shook his head. 'The hills only get higher and the canyons deeper. It looks like this is the end of the line.'

CHAPTER THREE

After the swim Dill Humminger and his riders had stopped in a sheltered canyon that led up from the river to the open plateau. There they had built a fire to dry themselves out, letting the Injun Creek cut drift on, Dill having no fear of not making the east-side ranch by night. They were still there when the first snowflake landed on the back of his hand. He suppressed an impulse to smile. The pair with him were part of a ring he had got together on OT. They knew he had put something over on Twig and why without being fully in his confidence. So he made no comment on the fine, bright crystal that melted slowly on the worn leather of his glove.

Walt Trumbull, long-legged and thick of trunk, was the next to notice the change in the air. He was lifting a cigarette to his mouth but stopped his hand and squinted up at the sky.

'Judah Brown's thingamabob knew what it was talkin' about,' he said.

Cass Pickering took a look at the black clouds and a grin spread over his face. 'It sure did. The bottom's gonna drop out up there.'

'And we better get movin',' Dill said.

He walked to his horse and swung into the saddle, privately congratulating himself. He had been on a routine trip to Injun Creek, with no intention of meeting the trail herd of feeders. Then, the morning before, the cold air had come howling down across the highlands of the Okanogan. He had been in the country long enough to know that something mean was headed their way, born of a polar disturbance. His hunch had turned to conviction when they reached Brown's Landing, and he saw how far the barometer had fallen. The one other time he had seen it drop so far so fast a howling blizzard had hammered the country for weeks. Since he had made a practice of rubbing Twig the wrong way for years, working him into a defiant frame of mind had been dead easy.

Dill hurried his men until they had caught up with the steers. Afterward he led the way, his helpers loosely working the easily handled little bunch. The canyon climbed on to the top, letting them out on the vast interior basin of the Columbia. The snow fell thickly by then, but Dill wasn't afraid of it. He knew the country well enough to ride it in the darkest night.

It was like a skillet, he had often thought, that covered most of eastern Washington. The Okanogan would be its handle, pressed into the highlands. The Columbia curved around its western edge, between the desert bottom and the Cascades foothills. The trail to which Twig had committed himself so brashly, and so obligingly as well, threaded between the hills and river over there. Dill knew he wouldn't want to be responsible for six hundred steers on that trail, the way it would soon be, although he was responsible for their being there.

Once out of the river depression, Dill twisted in the saddle to look back. His men were hunched in their saddles, snow nearly masking them from sight. The cattle were following him and willing to quicken their step. He increased it, taking them forward at a trotting walk that Oak would never stand for. But he had done a lot of things that Oak, if he knew, would bust a gusset about. Secluded by the snow and his forward position, Dill gave in to the impulse to laugh. No matter what had happened and was yet to come, Oak had only himself to blame.

The trail they now followed was the east branch of the old cattle trail to the Cariboo. He covered it as well as the west branch several times with Oak, himself barely grown then and full of the longings and the imaginings of the very young. He had caught Oak's eye, he knew, because he was the kid of the outfit, a range waif Oak had found and offered a job. While Oak had not played the role consciously – far from that – he was the closest to a father Dill ever had. He had wilted at Oak's displeasure, bloomed at his praise. He had worked overtime and double time to make sure he pulled his weight. He had won his spurs. For a while he had even fooled himself into thinking he had also won the closer relationship for which his young heart yearned.

Dill quit laughing, for he couldn't laugh and remember the day Oak got hurt on the bluffs over Okanogan Lake, far up the trail to the Cariboo. The stretch was known to be treacherous, so Oak had ridden ahead of the immense herd they were taking up to feel it out. On point behind him, Dill had been the nearest to him when Oak's horse lost its footing on the rotten shale and went rolling down the slide below. He hadn't been able to tell immediately what happened to Oak, and if ever he had experienced living death that was the time. He no longer remembered what he did, only that he found himself down there, too, his own safety forgotten. Oak lay there, crumpled but miraculously escaped from the saddle that had gone plummeting into the lake below with the horse.

He wondered if Oak ever thought of that and of the maverick who bent over him, unable to hold back his sobs. It was burned into Dill's brain forever. He could still see Oak open his eyes, hear him say weakly, 'It's all right, son. Hey, now. Pull in your lip.

Only bung up my leg a little.'

The leg had been hurt more than a little. The shattered hip had gone long before they got to medical help so it would be set, and it had never healed the way it should have. Ever afterward it hurt Oak so he couldn't mount a horse much less sit a saddle, and that kept him off all but the nearest, easiest to reach ranges. So somebody else had to do his foot and saddle work, and Dill had been the one chosen, for Twig had been only a button and of little use in the work and business end.

Dill hadn't resented Twig so much then, for Oak had called him 'Son,' that one time, too, although never again. So Dill had doubled his devotion to Oak and while he started out as a sort of errand boy he was soon the physical instrument by which Oak carried out the projections of his will. It was a will turned harder, grimmer, and more unyielding by his handicap. Eventually Dill was his acknowledged second in command.

But each year made changes in Twig, too, adding height, weight, and savvy. There came another day Dill would never forget. This was the one on which Oak said, 'I reckon it's time to put the boy to work. He's got a lot to learn before he'll be ready to take over from me. Which he'll have to. He's all I've got.'

Dill still wondered if he had flinched

openly as well as within himself. He hadn't been able to say anything.

'I'll do what I can,' Oak went on, 'but you'll have to teach him the kind of things I can't, Dill. Make a cowhand out of him. Then I'll try to make him a cowman as well.'

Dill had hated the years that followed, years in which he knew he was training a man to replace himself. They were years in which he also hated Oak for drawing that line between his hired man and his son. It was too painfully a difference that nothing on earth could change. But the habit of obeying Oak was ingrained. He had carried out his orders as far as the training went, faithfully but far more brutally than Twig had ever let his father know...

The snow whipped down on the drive all day, and icy winds tried to rip it to pieces. Yet the steers were steaming, for Dill crowded them without pity to make sure they reached Injun Creek grass by night. Even so, the light was gone by the time they entered the huge, crosswinds coulee that sheltered this ranch. Two more hours had passed before they reached its headquarters.

They had penned the steers, cared for the horses, and were walking into the cookshack when Pickering laughed. 'Well, here we are, snug as bugs in a rug. And I wonder what the son and heir's doin' about now.'

'Wishin' he'd listened instead of talked, I

bet,' Trumbull said. 'I'd sure like to be a mouse in the corner when Oak takes off his hide.'

He wouldn't mind sharing that corner, Dill thought. There was no doubt now that the Peshastin herd would wind up in serious trouble even if it wasn't wiped out. And that would be another instance of the impulsive irresponsible, muleheaded streak Oak had become convinced that his son possessed. Failings that had let Twig climb no higher in the chain of command than supervision of the trail work. Now there was somebody else to keep reminded of these flaws in Twig. A somebody who had opened the way to overcome the obstacle of not being Oak's own flesh and blood.

Dill awakened the next morning to be cast into doubt that Twig's plight would be as bad as he hoped. The snow had stopped in the night. In the early dawn stars shone brilliantly to suggest that the storm had ended much too soon. Yet the air, when he went outdoors, was colder than the day before. The light strengthened to show a coulee floor covered with snow. He saw that it came halfway to the knees of the animals in the fenced pasture. His good spirits returned. It would be worse over there by the mountains.

He was tempted to head in to report to Oak on the brush at the Okanogan and express his fears for the herd started down the west side against his advice. But it wouldn't do to seem eager to do so. He decided to visit the Rock and Crab Creek ranches and then go in. Then he would reach Wenatchee City about the time Twig would have got there if the trail had been good.

He struck out after breakfast, making his way through a foot of snow to the upper end of Moses Coulee. This was a grassed and watered trough that ran for some thirty miles to the southwest so that its right-hand rim was a good windbreak. Under the rim the snow was thin, and his horse made good time. He stayed in this formation until shortly after noon.

Then, at the Rock Creek mouth, he turned right along another depression of high, broken walls. The headquarters of the brood ranch were ten miles farther on, standing in the lee of a detached mountain. The afternoon was half gone by the time he reached there and found himself closeted with Trink Neysmith, the ranch foreman.

They were in Neysmith's cubbyhole office at one end of the cookshack. While he applied himself to food the cook had brought in, Dill began to realize that the foreman was worried.

'Something's eatin' on you, Trink,' he said, when Neysmith failed to explain his edginess. 'What?'

'Well–' Neysmith paused to rub his jaw. He was a gangling, hook-nosed man and one of those privy to things Dill now wished no one knew but himself. Neysmith ran a tongue along thin lips and went on uncomfortably, 'I oughtn't to tell tales outta school. Sid Lublin won't thank me for it, if he learns I did. I just happened to hear about it when Curly Dawson come up from Crab Creek, the other day. It's bothered me ever since.'

'What has?' Dill said impatiently.

Neysmith pulled in a hesitant breath, then plunged ahead finally. 'Well, it seems Lublin took it into his head he could slip out a cut of beef. To that butcher in Ruby that don't care who used to own the meat he sells. That breed Cultus Joe tried to sneak the stuff across the corner of the Injun reservation. He thought this would get him past Judah Brown's town. Then damned if he didn't run into Judah, anyhow. He'd been over to the agency about somethin'. Judah thought it looked queer. A hundred head of OT beef way off there, even if Cultus did show him a bill of sale made out to the butcher. What was queerer was Twig up in the Okanogan *buyin'* steers for OT at the very same time.'

'Damn Lublin,' Dill fumed. 'I told him to stay away from them mines.'

Dill felt his spine turn as cold as the outdoors. 'When did this happen?'

'About a week ago, according to Curly.'

'Too temptin', I reckon,' Neysmith said unhappily. 'You know he can't turn down an easy dollar. Trouble is, he's gonna get us all in a bind. Judah Brown's no injun.'

It was my name on that bill of sale, Dill thought worriedly. He said, 'I was goin' down to Crab Creek, anyhow. I'll put a stop to anymore of that.'

'You'll have to set on him hard to do it.'

Dill left Rock Creek the next morning at first light. He spent a long, cold day in the saddle, crossing Moses Coulee and striking over the plateau to the south end of Grand Coulee. Going on past Moses Lake, he came to the upper side of the Crab Creek country. Afterward the snow was less deep and let him make time. In late afternoon he saw the Frenchman Hills. He rode by them through a belt of dunes and dry channels to come, at nightfall, to the headquarters of the last of the east-side ranches.

On south lay OT's most isolated and, in many ways, its best range. This ran from Saddle Mountain to the mouth of Snake River in one direction. In the other it swept from the Columbia to Washtucna Coulee. All of it was desert, but it was covered with sand grass and white sage that was excellent, fattening winter feed for cattle. In the heart of the desert lay Twin Wells from which beef could be shipped all winter long by way of the new railroad to reach the market when beef was scarce and the prices high.

Unfortunately, as Dill now saw it, this prime beef could bring fancy prices in other markets, too. And the man running this ranch was the least to be trusted among those Dill had been forced to work with to carry out his private schemes.

Lublin had his own quarters, which Dill always shared. And Dill said nothing of what Neysmith had told him until they were sitting there, after supper, by the fire. He began mildly, 'Hear you sent some beef to Ruby, Sid.'

Lublin was short, stocky, and had a thatch of kinky black hair over a bulging brow. He nodded. 'Too good to pass up.'

'Hear Cultus Joe had to produce a bill of sale for Judah Brown to look at,' Dill added.

Lublin's eyes narrowed, and he said cautiously, 'Where'd you hear that?'

'I seen Judah at the landing,' Dill said, respecting Neysmith's desire to keep out of it. 'He was curious about it.'

Lublin's eyes went hard. 'Joe got careless, that's all.'

'That ain't all by a hell of a lot,' Dill snapped. 'How many more of them blank bills of sale, with my signature, do you have?'

'That was the last.'

'It had better be, seein' what a damned fool you are.'

Lublin's eyes flashed. 'Now, look here. Supposin' I told you I want a dozen more of the same. Which I'm thinkin' of tellin' you right now.'

'You threatening me?'

'We had a good thing,' Lublin said with a sudden, flat vehemence. 'Then you got this notion you can marry your way into Oak Tully's family. Mebbe you can and it'll fix you up fine. But how about the rest of us boys?'

Taken aback by what was a more sobering situation than he expected, Dill felt his heart quicken. 'I'll take care of you,' he muttered.

'Damned right you will.' Lublin's eyes raked him. Behind them was resentment, malevolence, and a festering suspicion. 'I been watchin' the change in you. This gal comes along, and all at once you got somethin' a lot more to your taste than us boys and what we helped you do. But you forget somethin' you better not forget for a minute. I can fix your wagon any time I want. You get high-handed with me, and that time has come.'

Dill had no comeback to that. If only he had waited. But he had never heard of Lorna Milne when his disgruntlement first drove him to take what he no longer hoped to be given by the man he had once worshiped. He covered his inability to answer by rolling a cigarette, thinking of what had

48

given Lublin this hold on him.

Until the railroad came through the best beef markets had been the mining camps springing up all around the cattle ranges. It had been those of the rich Coeur d'Alene that had tantalized him into taking the first fateful step. He had had the power to transact business for OT. Lublin knew that and had pointed out how easy it would be to make secret sales in the Coeur d'Alene. Its camps were not a hard drive from the east-side ranches. OT was doing no business there, as yet, its output still going north to the Cariboo and the Similkameen mines.

All that was needed to cover up was a little juggling of the books, the roundup tallies, the calf-crop figures, the natural die-off, and the inevitable losses to predators. Lublin had handled the deliveries, selling prime beef off the Crab Creek winter range. Dill had done nothing but furnish him with signed bills of sale, for Lublin's use, and doctor the book-keeping as required. The trouble was Lublin's end of it made it necessary to take several others on the east-side spreads into it. All of them knew about it now, and most were men who would see things like Lublin did and back him.

Dill saw no alternative to letting Lublin go ahead as he would, and that grew more dangerous every month. Bleeding OT couldn't be kept up indefinitely without finally becoming apparent. Even now, if Twig took over unexpectedly and ran the next round-up, incriminating discrepancies would show up. And Dill knew there would be no way to cover his own tracks.

He came out of his brooding to notice that Lublin was grinning as if reading his mind.

'So it won't be me and the boys you drop out of the game,' he said. 'And it won't be you that drops out. But there's somebody who'd give you what you're after, and a lot surer than the way you're goin' about it, if he dropped out. I could arrange it.'

'You can cut out that kind of talk,' Dill growled.

'Too temptin'?' Lublin said, and he laughed.

CHAPTER FOUR

It was about an hour after supper when Twig, pinned down for twenty-four hours in the trap, pricked up his ears. The sound was the first, other than the shrieking ground blizzard that had held them in camp all that day, that he had heard. The others alerted, too, when more sounds bored through the windy night. They were insistent, plaintive, like a distress call, although Twig didn't know much about river signals.

'Just be the down boat,' he decided. 'But it's sure late.'

'No wonder,' Ferd Darling pointed out. 'It's been a mean lay.'

Darling didn't exaggerate. The storm, which had dumped inches of new snow and whipped all of it into impassable drifts, had put a second seal on the doom of the cattle. Twig was no longer even sure he could save the horses, although they were much less helpless in deep snow that cattle. If he waited much longer, he might even lose his men, he thought. The punishment they had absorbed had begun to show, and they were dangerously low on food.

'Hey, that's thing's stopped,' Buck Shipley

said. 'It's us they're tryin' raise.'

That seemed to be true. The signals kept coming and from the same point on the river. Twig hadn't even wondered if the storm had forced the steamers to tie up. This was the first place they had reached that was close enough to see one go by. And the wind hadn't gone down enough for the air to clear until that night. 'They must be able to see our fire,' he said. 'Maybe they got themselves hung up on a shoal and need help. Come on.'

It was easier to plow through the snow on foot than to saddle their tired, hungry horses and make them do it. The calls still came steadily and seemed to originate at the mouth of the gulch. The trail outfit plunged off in that direction, and before long Twig could make out the steamer's lights. When he turned to look back at the camp he was sure the firelight could be seen from the river. They were wanted, although it was hard to believe anybody could be in worse trouble than they.

The shore along there was high and rocky, with an abrupt drop to the water. They reached it to see that the packet was the *Chief*, Abner Brown's command. It had nosed in above a gravel bar below them and was held there precariously by a slowly turning wheel. Yet the boat didn't seem to be in trouble.

There were a couple of men on the fore-deck but it was Abner's voice that boomed out at them.

'You fellers hung up?'

He was in the pilothouse, Twig saw, where he had dropped open a window. The dim light behind him outlined another figure, that of a woman. Melissa, Twig realized. She'd had her visit out and was returning to her agent's job at Wenatchee City.

'We thought you were,' Twig called back.

'That you, OT?' Abner answered in surprise.

'Us and six hundred steers.'

'Well, I'll be blamed. We seen firelight and thought it was stranded travelers we could pick up. I sure hoped that you'd got past the head. When I went up yesterday it sure looked mean.'

'It looks even meaner now.'

'I reckon so.' Abner was silent a moment. 'I can give you men a lift, but I don't know what I could do for the steers.'

Twig didn't know, either. Even if the bank permitted loading, and Abner had no freight and passengers, he couldn't pick up more than handful of the herd. Twig turned to the men with him. 'If any of you want to take him up on that, I sure won't blame you.'

They didn't even seem to hear him.

'Well, I can't hang here any longer,' Abner

called. 'Luck to you, if that's any help.'

He pulled up the window, a gong sounded loudly, and then Twig watched the steamer back out. It slipped around the bar and headed on downstream, soon to be lost in the frigid darkness except for winking fireflies of light. Their last link with the outer world went with it. Twig looked at his men. He should have ordered them to go. Yet he knew they wouldn't have done it unless he went, too, and he hadn't been able to bring himself to abandon the steers to their fate.

'You're a bunch of knotheaded mules,' he said. 'But thanks.'

They trudged back to camp and had hardly bedded down when the wind started another go at the country.

An hour later it was scooping and throwing snow harder than it had that day. Twig accepted it, but the hope that the men's loyalty had lifted in him was running out. What if they did work a miracle and get past the barrier? There would be no feed to keep life in a herd already half dead of starvation. Yet, after the support he had been given, he would hang and rattle.

By daylight conditions were so bad that they dared not leave camp because of the danger of losing their bearings. The day was nearly gone before the wind grew silent enough for them even to hear the complaining cattle above them in the gulch. But then as the air grew calmer the snow mists cleared. Twig saw that he had time before dark to look into a possibility that had occurred to him in his desperation.

Without telling the men what he was up to, he left the camp and scuffed his way on foot to the river. It was tough going, but he eventually found himself at the spot where Abner Brown had held the steamer. A margin of ice thirty to forty feet wide had formed in the intense cold. It ran in both directions as far as he could see. Beyond the ice the current looked fatally cold and swift. Yet if the ice would hold a few steers at a time, and if the footing didn't prove too slippery, they might make it around the head that way. A little upstream was a place where he thought the cattle could get down to the ice. It was probably the most fool-hardy of his many muleheaded under-takings, but he decided to try it in the morning.

Somewhere in the night even this reckless resort became impossible. They came awake as one man at the new sound carried from the distance. This one was an ominous rumble that built up to a steady, grinding roar. It seemed to last for minutes, and the silence in the camp that followed for min-utes more.

Then Ashley broke it, lifting his head from

the pillow to say thickly, 'Snowslide. Guess where.'

It couldn't be anywhere but at the bald face of Quibble Mountain, which was the only precipitous surface near them. So there would be no passing below on the ice. That would already be broken under countless tons of snow. Yet the slide might have changed the face of things on the mountain itself.

Twig clung to this stubbornly and was out in the first light to see. Except for a lingering, foggy effect the air was clear. The wind for the time being was nothing to worry about. And when he reached the point he stopped his horse to stare upward at changes surpassing his own guesses. The slide had torn itself loose almost at the top, and the rock up there was bare. The lower half of the face was piled with the spent avalanche at an angle much less abrupt than before, and this more gently tilted surface looked stable. It was possible that a new trail could be broken along the upper edge, where the snow gave way to the bare rock. If so, he could forget the old and still deeply buried one.

The new trail would be awesomely high on the face. The cattle might be so weak they could never make the climb, even if they could be prodded into trying. If they made it up there, tricky stepping would be necessary to get them across. Once across, there still would be no feed between there and the Wenatchee Valley. But it was a chance, the only one left to save the cattle.

Twig worked back up the gulch, following the edge of the headland, and then drove his horse into virgin snow that was belly-deep on the horse. He rode at a slant to minimize the effort of climbing, and after a short distance the snow had been scoured away until it wasn't so deep. He rose slowly higher, picking his way, yet the underfed horse was soon heaving and blowing steam. After what seemed a long time they were at the top of the slide. The footing there was better.

He let the horse blow for several minutes, himself feeling dizzy and jittery and all too aware that if the snow beneath him started to move his troubles were over forever. Presently he struck out across the face, going slow and taking pains. The trail he broke had to be where bare rock supported the weight, with the snow only edging it to keep the horse and later the cattle from slipping. It worked, at least for the horse, and when he had crossed the face Twig went on to check the south side of the headland. The slope there was gentler, he found, and he came down on the regular trail without much trouble. The obstacle was behind him but far, as yet, from being behind the cattle.

He was about to start back across the headland and return to camp when something he sighted down the river stopped him in his tracks. Far in the distance, and so dwarfed as to seem a toy, a steamboat was out, and men were working back and forth. He didn't know what to make of it and decided to go down there and find out.

By the time he reached the steamer he knew it was the *Chief* and that it was unloading baled hay on the beach. Abner Brown stood on the deck watching the operation. He had his pipe in his mouth and had seen Twig without paying him any attention. The hay was nearly gone from the deck, but there was a pile of it ashore that made Twig's mouth water.

Riding up to them, he yelled, 'Hey. Who you leavin' that there for?'

Abner took the pipe from his mouth. 'Well, at the feed yard,' he called back, 'it was charged to OT.'

'It's mine?'

'Providin' you agree to pay charter charges,' Abner said with a grin. 'I had to give up a run for this.'

Pay charter charges? Twig would have given the man the blood in his veins. Yet there was a possible bug in the bedroll, and he said, 'Oak arrange this?'

Abner shook his head. 'Melissa. She worried about them steers all the way down

58

the river the other night. She said if you couldn't get 'em to hay, maybe we could get hay to them. Should've got Oak's permission, all right. But she said you looked stupid enough already and told the feed store it was you who ordered it.'

Twig dismounted and went up the gangplank, hardly able to believe in the hay let alone what Melissa had done to help him not only get out of the bind but to save face. Abner had even more to tell him. He had started up the day before, he said, and had made dumps a day's drive apart all the way up from Wenatchee City. He had had to make the last drop here because of the bluff at the mouth of the gulch beyond Quibble. He had intended to go on up with the boat, hoping they could find a place upstream where the steers could be loaded. Then they could be taken aboard in small lots and ferried down to the first hay.

Twig told him there might be a much faster way and explained the snowslide and how he hoped to trail the steers over. 'If they can't make it, we'll drag hay to 'em till they've got enough strength. Believe me, Abner, what you've done already is a favor I'll never forget.'

'As a favor to us, though,' Abner said, 'don't let it get out that Melissa took it on herself. It was way out of line. After all, you *could* have ordered it when we seen you the other night.'

'And was too stupid to do it,' Twig agreed. 'Just like she thought.'

He smiled to himself. Melissa knew she hadn't done anything anybody could fault her for. She had just been afraid that honesty would make him give her credit for it, and she wanted to save his pride as bad as he wanted it saved. So she had told Abner to say what he had said. Twig wouldn't lie, but he wouldn't go out of his way to correct anybody's impression that he had figured this out himself.

With the hay unloaded and the weather showing signs of improving, Abner was anxious to get back into his regular runs. Twig tried to thank him and was motioned silent. So Twig went ashore, and the gangplank was pulled aboard. In a few minutes the little packet was moving out into the channel and turning for the downstream run. Twig mounted and headed for camp. He felt as good as the steers would feel when they could get at the hay.

It took a good part of that day to move the cattle out of the gulch. The crew rode back and forth across the head half a dozen times before they tried it with animals, breaking down more snow and packing it harder. Then the horse band was taken over without a hitch. A cut of ten of the stronger steers followed. They didn't like the idea, balked, and tried to turn back, but finally they got it through their heads that they had to cross. Twig had sent men ahead to scatter the hay and break open the bales. Once the cattle got a whiff of it, they needed no advice from the punchers.

By the next morning the hay was gone, but Twig had a stronger herd, and there would be feed at each camp until they came into the Wenatchee. The trail hands were as cheered as Twig, although they were by then on leaner rations than their charges. They trailed out early and, two days later, were sure of making the valley by night. The trail had become easy to travel, so in mid-afternoon Twig rode on ahead of the drive.

The Wenatchee's valley was very much a repetition of the Okanogan, although it ran west from the Columbia instead of north. It had been a favorite campground of the Indians, who had fished for salmon at the falls and lent the region their name. Later, cattle drives to and from Canada had used it, and miners had worked the bars. Now the valley was taken up by cattle ranches, with a few farms sprinkled in. Wenatchee City was its trading center and only town.

The trail from the Kittitas Valley, and the railroad there at Ellensburg, came into the Wenatchee by way of the Peshastin. Oak's first ranch had been set up on this latter stream where it joined the upper Wenatchee

River, and this was still OT's hay ranch. Even after the east-side ranches were added, the Peshastin had been Oak's home, as well as Twig's, until Oak moved to town after he was hurt. Now Oak lived in town with the ward who was his companion, housekeeper, and substitute for the daughter he never had.

It took only a couple hours traveling to bring Twig to the town. There he rode onto a street parallel to the river and lined with false-front buildings. The snow was only a few inches deep there, for the valley was protected by the bare hills on the north side. The plank walk joining the business fronts had been shoveled and scuffed clear. On the river side of the street were the ferry landing, the wharf boat and office of the Brown Line, and a boatyard. The *Nixon* was up from Pasco, the new town down the Columbia, and tied to its own landing.

Twig turned at the one offshoot of the street onto an uncertain road and went on between rows of leafless trees and weathered dwellings. The house at whose gate he stopped was the largest in town. A two-story wooden structure, it was overhung by massive trees under which countless Indians had camped. Twig had an Indian's stony face when, swinging down, he glanced toward it. He never looked forward to his reports to Oak, although none had been as bad as the one he had to make. The doors of the stable were shut, so he couldn't see if Oak's buggy was there or gone. He trailed reins and went up the graveled path to the porch, swinging himself with a jauntiness he didn't feel.

This house was supposed to be his home, too, but he always had a feeling when he came to it that he ought to knock on the door. He stifled the impulse once more, pushed open the door, and stepped into a warm hallway. The sitting room on the left, where he usually found Oak, showed nobody at all.'

'Hey,' he yelled. 'Anybody here?'

A girl's voice answered from the back of the house. 'There sure is.' Then it sharpened in inquiry, 'Twig? Is it *you?*'

It sure wasn't Dill, if she had been hoping to see him. And then Lorna appeared in the kitchen doorway at the far end of the hall. If she had been let down she recovered quickly and came toward him smiling. Twig didn't say a word, watching her and wishing that either she wasn't so all-fired pretty or that she would let him know where he stood. She was a tall girl, dark and sinuous, and the pink in her cheeks suggested that she was starting supper. Oak was probably in the kitchen, drinking coffee and watching her work. He liked to do that, and what man wouldn't, Twig thought.

Lorna gave him both her hands and said

warmly, 'Well, you took the breath out of me. I didn't expect to see you after what I heard.'

So Dill had got in and made his own variety of hay out of what had happened at the Okanogan. Twig let go of her hands and said gruffly, 'Where's Oak?'

'He drove up to the Peshastin as soon as the storm would let him. You know how he worries about the stock in bad weather.' Lorna had a warm, low-pitched voice that Twig always seemed to hear with his heart as much as his ears. 'Come back into the kitchen. I'm starting supper, and you can eat with me. I hate to eat by myself.'

'Thanks. I thought Oak'd be here, and I'd better check in. But I've got to get back to the herd and find a place to hold it tonight.'

Lorna stared at him and said sharply, 'Herd?'

'What do you think we trailed down from the Okanogan? A flock of turkeys?'

'Why – I took it for granted that you'd abandoned the herd.'

Twig wasn't a bit surprised, but he pretended to be. 'Why, what made you think that?'

'Well, Dill came through this morning from Crab Creek. And he said—' She broke off as if not wanting him to know that she got as many bad reports on him as Oak did.

'I know what he said. Where's he now?'

'He went on up to see Oak.'

Twig shrugged. He had had little hope of getting to Oak first, anyway. He knew Lorna was deeply puzzled as to how he had got the cattle through, but he didn't enlighten her. He didn't want to leave her yet, though, and amended his refusal of her invitation to supper, saying, 'I could use a cup of coffee before I go. We've been out of it the last few days. Got any made?'

She at least seemed glad that he wouldn't rush right off. She smiled and said, 'When don't I have, when Oak's usually here and drinking it all day. Come on.'

Twig followed her down the hallway into the kitchen where a fire crackled merrily in the big old range. He sat down at the table while Lorna brought cups of coffee and sat down across. She smiled at him, and it was a lovely smile. Her mother had been an old love of Oak, over in Nevada where Oak had cut his teeth in the cattle business.

This was a chapter in his father's life that Twig didn't know much about. But three years earlier Lorna's mother had died, leaving her alone and without means. So Oak, a widower, had offered her a home and taken her into his heart until she was much closer to him than Twig had been since he was a small boy. She returned the devotion serving Oak in the unquestioning way that

65

Dill did. Maybe that was why she seemed to be leaning toward Dill recently, although she was Twig's own age and much younger than Dill.

Lorna broke into and yet seemed to verify his thoughts by saying, 'I'm glad you got through with those feeders. Just the same you were contrary and reckless again. Sometimes I wonder if you'll ever grow up.'

'That's exactly what Dill wants you to think,' Twig retorted. 'What he wants Oak to think, too.'

She looked surprised. 'Why should he? He's only thinking of OT.'

'You bet he's thinking of OT.' For the first time since his trail problems started, Twig thought of what Judah Brown had tried to get across to him at the landing. 'And how much better he likes it without somebody around who could check up on him closer than Oak can.'

Lorna's mouth dropped open. 'Why – what on earth do you mean by that?'

'I mean Dill's made it his business for years to keep me in Dutch with my dad.'

'That's ridiculous.'

'And I would have thought so, too, till lately.' Twig got to his feet. 'How you fixed for stovewood?'

'Dill filled up the back porch this morning.'

'He would. Well, thanks for the coffee.'
Twig went down the hallway for his coat
and hat.

CHAPTER FIVE

Twig rejoined the herd while it came curving into the valley under the snow-splashed northern hills. Another day's drive remained to reach the Peshastin, but from there on he would have no trail problems to complicate the one again filling his mind. Just before dark he and the crew threw the steers into the feed lot of a settler who made a business of supplying drivers and at a reasonable price. The settler's wife gave them their first full meal since they got into the trap, and the trail crew bedded down comfortably in the barn.

In spite of the improved conditions, Twig found himself unready for the sleep that so quickly claimed the others. Hotheaded again, he had said more to Lorna than he should have, but what he had said still carried the ring of truth. In addition to harboring the jealousy Twig had long recognized, Dill was afraid of him. No wonder he went at a trot to keep his fences mended.

Not until that night did Twig realise the danger he was in. Dill not only could keep him from getting too much authority on the ranch, he could, if it was important enough to him, bring about a final and total break with his family. Only now was Twig glimpsing how important to Dill OT was and how everything stood in the man's favor.

Oak's temper could be manipulated the same as the son's had been. The chronic distrust Dill had already built up in him was a good seedbed for a sudden, violent quarrel, unforgivable and unforgiven. If that came about, neither of them would back down, and Twig would no more stay on the ranch than Oak would want him to stay. The next step made Twig flinch, but it was possible. If Oak lost the son he seemed set against recognizing as he really was, he might well adopt Lorna, who had always delighted and never displeased him in the least way. So if Dill managed to marry her, he might be marrying OT, too, permanently covering the snake tracks he had made and putting himself in clover, besides.

Dill had to be stopped. That was all there was to it.

The temperature rose markedly during that last night on the trail, leaving no doubt that the cold spell was over for the time being. Fed, watered, and no longer punished, the cattle were easy to handle. So it was only four in the afternoon when the herd reached the Peshastin and followed up an old miners' trail to the ranch headquarters at the edge of the mountains. The buildings stood in a grove of bare old trees, and out from them ran a fenced bottom-land. Twig helped his men throw the cattle into this, and then they rode in.

When their horses had been taken care of, the men headed immediately for the cook-shack and supper. With less enthusiasm, Twig went on to the old frame house. Oak was there, seated at the open fire and smoking a cigar that he drew on wordlessly while he watched his son come into the room. He had been and still was a more heavily built man than Twig. His seamy face was square-jawed, and his shock of gray hair was as thick as it had ever been. This was their first meeting in over a month, but his only greeting was a hardly detectable nod of the head.

Twig knew that Dill's report wasn't the whole cause of the chill. Seeing him so soon had made Oak believe, as it had Lorna at first, that he had abandoned the cattle in the trap his folly had carried them into and come on lightheartedly. In that same frigid moment of meeting, Twig saw something else. He was going to let Oak have the quarrel Dill wanted so badly to come off. But he would do it in cold blood rather than hotheaded rashness, keeping it more under control and, God willing, its consequences less enduring.

He hung up his hat and coat and walked over to the fireplace. Turning his back to the heat, he took another long look at Oak, then said with deceptive serenity, 'Where's Dill?'

'Why, over in the bunkhouse, I reckon.'

'I guess he told you he met me at Brown's Landing, and we had a difference of opinion.'

'He told me.' Oak took the cigar from his mouth and waited. When Twig didn't add anything he said, letting his anger flow into his voice, 'And where did you leave 'em?'

'Why, out there in the holding pasture.'

Oak came forward, his big hands gripping the arms of his wheelchair. 'Holding pasture? How many?'

'Why, all of 'em,' Twig said.

'What're you tryin' to give me?' Oak tossed the cigar into the fire and stared at his son disbelievingly. 'Word come down before I left town that the trail is plugged tight at Quibble.'

'It sure was,' Twig said easily. 'But we made it all right.'

Oak was too angry to let go of it and give way to relief, let alone to feel pride in his son for having tackled and licked a tough problem. 'Then it was fool's luck,' he snorted. 'Dill told me what the situation was and what he wanted you to do. Why the hell didn't you do it?'

'I did what he wanted me to do, Oak. I come down the west side. The only thing he wanted that I didn't do was lose the herd.

The feeders are here where you wanted 'em and not eatin' up the feed at Injun Creek.'

The wind had gone out of Oak's sails, finally, as it would go out of Dill's when he heard the feeders had come through. But Oak's reason for feeling deflated was different from Dill's. He had worried about those steers and even more about the apparent irresponsibility that had put them in danger. He had built up a head of steam he had intended to blow off now, only to find himself without much reason.

He listened moodily to Twig's account of the storm-harried drive. If he hadn't been nursing his temper he might have seen a likeness to some of the winter-threatened drives to the Cariboo he still liked to talk about. He might even have seen a tenacity in his son like that which had made those drives and gone on to build OT. As it was, the good points went, as usual, completely unseen.

'It was still fool's luck,' he growled, lighting a fresh cigar. 'And what did you mean by your remark that Dill wanted you to lose the steers?'

'What would you have done if I had?'

'I'd have taken you off your job, that's what.'

Twig nodded. 'And that's what I meant by my remark.'

Oak had something he could fuel his

temper with, finally. Leaning forward, he said, 'Now, you look here. Dill's got more'n a few years age on you. He learned this business under conditions a hell of a lot tougher than you ever see. You get that through your head, and when it comes to things he knows more about than you do, you listen. You hear me?'

'Or what, Oak?' Twig said softly.

'Or, by God, I'll give him back authority you can't dispute and ignore.'

'Which is what he's been working for ever since you took it away from him.'

'Horse sweat. It's a case of a soft kid gettin' too big for his britches and needin' to be cut down to size.'

Oak's glare convinced Twig that he wouldn't listen for a minute to what Judah Brown had hinted at, as Judah himself had realized. Dill had done a good job, for he had worked overtime at it while the man he was slowly destroying was only now sensing the truth. Twig looked at Oak for a long moment, hoping to see a trace of relenting. There was none, and he swung and left the house.

It would be solely up to him to dig into the mystery behind Judah's hints. The best way to do it would be to make Dill think he had got what he wanted at last, then watch and see what he did with his success. Twig felt his shoulders pull up while he walked across a ranch yard grown dark. Coming down the west side, he had, for once, been wholly his own man. Now that it had come off successfully, looking back on it made him feel damned good. And, win or lose, it would be good to do something more that way. Like rubbing Dill's nose in it again.

Dill slept in the bunkhouse, but as range boss he rated a separate room. Twig went through its door without warning and shut it behind him with a shove. Dill was playing solitaire in the saffron light of an oil lamp. He looked up in annoyance, thinking it was one of the hired hands breaking in on his privacy. The expression changed to one of ill-concealed triumph when he saw who it was. Shut up in here, Twig realized, Dill hadn't heard yet that the feeders were all out in the pasture and not much the worse for wear.

'Well,' Dill grunted. 'You managed to save your own hide, anyway.'

'I suppose you're set to send a skinnin' crew up to try and salvage the others.'

'I guess there'd be a question of whether that's the range boss's or the trail boss's job.'

'It's all yours now, Dill. I'm not the trail boss, anymore.'

Elation leaked out of Dill like sweat cracking through his skin. He tried to keep it hidden by running through a few more cards. 'So he finally fired you. Too bad, but you brought it on yourself.'

'With plenty of help from you.'

Dill looked up again, brazenly confident. 'Me? How do you figure that?'

'I don't have to figure. It's all there, built into Oak's mind, and every bit of it come to him secondhand. Through you. He couldn't get out to see for himself. I couldn't argue when I didn't know what you were tellin' him. I couldn't point out places where I was pretty good. He'd have batted my ears down for braggin'. So you could build up an image in his mind nothin' like I really am.'

'I gave him the bad with the good,' Dill retorted. 'That's how he wanted it.'

'I know there was bad. Some of it was plain mistakes. Most of it you foxed me into like you thought you were foxin' me up there on the Okanogan.'

'Sure,' Dill jeered. 'You lose him a lot of money then try to blame me. But if he took your job away from you, I don't guess it worked.'

Dill was feeling so good, it was a pleasure to let him have both barrels. 'You're wrong twice there. I never lost Oak a damned cent. Every steer I left Brown's Landing with is out there in the holding pasture, right this minute. And Oak didn't take the job away from me. He don't even know yet that I've quit.'

Dill put down the deck of cards and

leaned back, his staring eyes canted up at Twig. It took him a moment to gather what had been said, and his mouth worked soundlessly. Twig's eyes never left him, and he knew he was looking at a frightened man, not one disgruntled because a sneaky trick hadn't come off.

'What're you tryin' to pull?' Dill said in a dull voice. 'What are you up to?'

Twig had stirred up that fear to be sure it was there. The next thing was to throw Dill off the track. 'Nothing in particular. I just don't know if I want to be in the cattle business or something else. I never had a chance to find out. I'm going to make that chance. And it looks like you're gonna win your dirty fight by default.'

'But what're you going to do?'

'I don't even know that.'

Twig heeled around and strode out. The men in the big outer room had heard voices grow angry, and they watched him curiously, particularly the ones in his trail crew – or in the trail crew that, only moments before, had been his. Twig remembered their loyalty and for a moment regretted what he had to do. But if they knew why he did it, he was sure they'd approve. He wished he could tell them, but the impression he left here had to be that he and Oak had finally locked horns for the last time.

It was harder going back to Oak than it

had been to face him the first time. Luckily old Henry was there putting a fresh log on the fire. The Chinese had cooked for OT since the early trail days and now remained as a pensioner and Oak's devoted attendant when Oak was at the Peshastin. Henry nodded at Twig, saying nothing because he was aware of the tension that had charged the room the instant Twig entered.

Oak still sat in his wheelchair, but the cigar in his fingers was as dead as his eyes. Twig knew that what he had to do would give him much less satisfaction than he had felt when he confronted Dill. Riled as he had been so many times, he had never completely forgotten what life must be like for Oak. A man who once had been so virile and active and now couldn't get off the seat of his pants without help.

Henry finished poking up the fire and slipped away. Oak still didn't act like he knew his son had come into the room, but Twig knew he did. So before he said anything himself, Twig went over to the rack beside the door and took down his coat and hat. Then he turned to look at his father.

He managed to keep his voice steady. 'I won't be around for a while, Oak. Maybe for quite a while. It all depends.'

Oak's glance shot up from the floor and swung onto him. Twig saw his chest swell as he sucked in a breath. Oak growled, 'I don't recollect givin' time off.'

'You didn't. I'm quitting. I'm just clearing out.'

Oak must have been afraid of something like that and set his mind to meet it. For his eyes hardened, and he said instantly, 'Don't think threats're gonna make me take back what I said about puttin' Dill back in charge. You ought to know I don't bluff and I can't be bluffed.'

'I know that, Oak, and it's the same with me. I'm quitting.'

'Because you got your dignity tromped on.'

'No. I'm of age, and I've got the right to quit. You had a chance to find out who you are, but you never gave me one. And I figure on finding out.'

'That ain't all.' Oak's voice was harsh. He cleared his throat, then took time to light his cigar, but that was to cover something on his face he didn't want Twig to see. 'You never appreciated what OT is. It all come too easy for you. But if you had half an inkling of what I had to put into it, you might have tried harder to measure up to your responsibilities.'

'I tried.'

Oak said nothing, clearly not believing that. When he finally spoke it was in a voice less angry than tired. 'All right. Get out of here. And when you find out what you

78

throwed away, don't come whinin' back.'

That was more than Twig had expected to hear, and the words cut through him like knives. In a moment of awful clarity he knew that he and Oak had the same complaint to make about each other. He had never been recognized for the person he was and had tried to be. For a terrible moment Twig thought he was going to reverse himself. But Dill had made that impossible. He had ingratiated himself with Oak so solidly, Oak would never think of checking up on him. Oak would be harder to convince of guilt in Dill than any jury.

Twig's own words were flat but as sure-tongued as his eyes had become clear-seeing. 'I wish you hadn't gone that far, Oak.'

Oak didn't say a word. Twig turned toward the door and left.

Without cattle to shove, it was hardly a three hour ride down the valley to Wenatchee City. Yet by the time Twig reached there Oak's town house was dark and locked for the night. He didn't want to get Lorna out of bed, but he knew he should. If he went on without seeing her, she would form her opinion of his actions from Dill even more than from Oak. So he rode in on the graveled drive and dismounted under the trees.

That put him close to her downstairs bedroom, and he picked up a pebble and tossed it against the window. He did this twice more before he saw her obscured shape beyond the glass. The sash came up an inch or so, and she called out cautiously.

'Twig? That you? Is something wrong?'

'Nothin' to get alarmed about,' he told her. 'I got something to tell you, if you don't mind me coming in.'

She hesitated, and it occurred to him that he had never been alone there with her at night, although he had more of a family right to be there than she did. She didn't say anything, but the sash slid closed and her vague shape vanished. He went around to the back door, which was nearest. By the time he got there a lamp had been lighted in the kitchen. Lorna unlocked the door for him.

'You scared me,' she said. 'Visitors at night can mean bad news. Is Oak all right?'

'Sure.'

Her thick dark hair hung in braids now. She had put a robe on over her nightdress, and her feet were in woolly slippers. His breath caught so that he couldn't get started on telling her. He had wanted her almost from his first acquaintance, yet it had never hit him like it did now. The knowledge that he might be handing her over to Dill raked him as hard as Oak's telling him if he left he wasn't to come back.

He said breathlessly, 'Golly, Lorna. You're sure beautiful.'

'You wake me up to tell me that?' she said, but she was pleased. 'And are you hungry?'

It came to him that he had been on the Peshastin and left it without once thinking of his supper. He could have used a bite, but her kitchen fire was out and he didn't want to bother her. 'I didn't leave the Peshastin till after supper,' he said evasively.

'Where you going now?'

'I don't know.' He couldn't dodge it any longer and plunged into it. 'You'll hear all about it, but I wanted to tell you myself. Oak and me had a go-round. Dill and me another. I've quit. I'm leavin' OT.'

'Oh, Twig.' She looked as exasperated a she was surprised. 'Why? You know you did a foolish thing and that you had a calling down coming to you. You turn your horse around and go right back up there and admit you did. You hear?'

'Too late for that. Oak told me not to come back.'

Lorna's slim young body slumped. He knew she was already on Oak's side, and that put her on Dill's automatically. In a way, Oak used her like he had his son to compensate for his own physical limitations. She not only kept him company and took care of his house, she ran his local errands and often drove for him when he went somewhere in his buggy. Maybe it was easier for a woman to subordinate herself, to be mindless and an instrument for serving somebody she had attached herself to. At least Lorna thrived on it.

She said, very faintly, 'So it's that bad.'

'Bad? It's the first self-respectin' move I ever made.' Then Twig thought of the drive he had made successfully against Dill's advice and amended that to, 'I mean it's the second.'

Her eyes hardened, and she said, 'What's jealousy got to do with self-respect?'

He might have known. It had been a cinch that she would paste that label on what he had said to her on his way up to the Peshastin. Despair silenced him, although there had been a slight chance that her feeling for Oak would make her listen if he had explained that a man Oak trusted *might* be dishonest and treacherous. And that a man she would possibly marry *might* hope to gain a lot more than a pretty wife. But Lorna's ears would be as deaf to that as Oak's, and nothing would open either pair of ears but proof.

He had never felt so tired and discouraged, but he said mildly, 'Call it what you like. But I've got to do it, and I hope you'll remember I looked at it that way. Remember and – well, not deal me clean out of your life, too.'

Lorna glanced away, her face dark,

troubled, and unrelenting. 'You walk out on Oak,' she said in a heavy voice, 'and you walk out on me.'

He nodded his acceptance. 'Sorry I disturbed your rest. Good night.'

She still hadn't looked at him when he closed the door behind him and walked out into the night.

CHAPTER SIX

The Brown Line wharf boat, bobbing in the slack water of the Columbia below the town, was more than a freight and passenger depot. Across one end of its huge barge house was a living quarters as compact as those aboard the steamboats. Melissa Brown lived there. Since either the *Arrow* or the *Chief* was tied up on that end of the run every night, she had one or the other of her gangling brothers to give her company most of the time.

Twig didn't go to her quarters as part of a plan. Riding away from Oak's town house, he came onto the town's main street to see nothing but dark windows except for a couple of saloons and the lobby of the hotel. He had meant to take a room at the hotel and get some rest before he decided on his next move. But a glance down toward the landing showed him that the *Chief* was there that night, with some of its windows still showing light. He owed a great deal to that boat and its master and its master's sister. He took his horse to the livery barn and had it put up, then walked down to the landing.

He knew the setup well enough not to go

aboard the packet. And when he knocked on the private door at the end of the wharf boat, it was Abner Brown who came in response. Abner's solemn features stirred in a grin. 'Well, howdy. Never expected to see you. Come on in.'

Twig stepped into a living room tight and neat as a steamboat cabin, and Abner shut the door. Melissa sat in a round-back chair, looking at him in surprise and with guarded eyes. There was color in her cheeks, like his coming there had embarrassed her. She had given him plenty of curryings only to turn around and do him a tremendous favor, and he guessed she didn't want him to read anything into the latter. He went to the chair Abner waved him to and sat down with his hat in his lap.

He looked at Melissa so straight she dropped her eyes. 'I already tried to thank Abner,' he said. 'And told him to thank you. But it's something I wanted to do again, in person.'

She was fussed and said, 'Well, nobody likes to see–'

'I know,' Twig said, grinning at her. 'Dumb critters sufferin' because of dumber people.' She had to smile at that, and when she did she was as pretty as Lorna. 'I'm sure grateful, Melissa. If it hadn't been for you two, I'd have been demoted to ridin' fence.'

'We turned a profit on it,' she said. 'Wait

till you get the freight bill.'

'I won't be there to see it.'

Melissa looked at him quickly, and Abner cut him an even sharper glance, but neither said anything.

'When I was at Brown's landing,' Twig went on 'your dad hinted that he had reason to think OT's being cheated on by its own hired help. Do either of you know what he meant by that?'

'If we did,' Abner said, shaking his head, 'and it's somethin' Judah didn't want to tell you, we wouldn't tell you either.'

'I know that. But I figured it might be different now that I've quit OT.'

'Quit?' Melissa gasped. 'I thought if you got the cattle through, you'd be all right.'

After that she couldn't deny she had done it for him and not the steers. That made him feel good, and it didn't look like they had disliked each other nearly as much as he had thought for so long.

'I was, as far as that went,' he told her. 'It went back farther than that. And it spread out partly to include the man your dad had in mind when he talked to me at the landing. A man who sure would have been pleased if you two hadn't got me out of my fix.'

Melissa was loosened up now. 'Dad never said anything to me about him, but I know you mean Dill Humminger. The whole country knows how he hates you and why. He used to act like it was him who owned OT, not Oak Tully. And he still thinks he ought to be the second in line.'

'He sure does,' Twig agreed. 'And it looks like that's where he stands, right now.'

'You gonna let him stay there?' Abner asked.

'Not if I can help it.'

Melissa's smile came again, warm and approving. Abner expressed his feelings with a teeth-showing grin.

Leaning forward, Abner said eagerly, 'Good for you. Ain't that what you say, Sis?'

'It sure is,' Melissa agreed. 'But how are you going to do it, Twig?'

'Plagued if I know, right now.'

'Look,' Abner said. 'Why don't you take a run up the river with me? Judah likes your cut, and he sure don't like Humminger. If he knew you've quit OT and why, he'd help you all he could. That could be a lot or a little.'

'I will. What time do you shove off in the morning?'

'Daylight,' Abner said. 'But don't worry about that. Sleep aboard tonight.'

'You've got yourself a passenger.'

They said good night, and when he was alone Twig stood motionless for a moment, a little scared by the step he had taken but at least feeling free and his own man. Then he undressed, blew out the lamp, and went to bed.

He slept so soundly that when he awakened the *Chief* was already on its way up the river. He grinned at the ceiling and lay there, lazy and feeling no guilt because of it. But he finally got up, washed in the chilly water in the pitcher on the stand, and dressed. When he looked out the cabin window he couldn't figure out where they were. From the water all the landmarks looked different, as strange as if he had never seen them before. But he knew they would be somewhere in Rocky Reach.

He put on his coat and hat and stepped out into the wind blowing across the texas. Moving forward against this, he saw Abner in the pilothouse, standing braced to the wheel. He slid open the door and stepped in.

'That you?' Abner said without taking his eyes off the water.

'Me.'

'Better go below and get your breakfast. I told the crew about you. They'll make you cozy.'

'I'm not used to being cozy, but thanks.'

'How do you like your boat ride?'

'Well, I never knew this river was so wide and deep and fast,' Twig confessed. 'It makes me uneasy.'

'That's the feelin' I get on a horse,' Abner said with a laugh. 'Go eat, then maybe I'll let you take the wheel a spell.'

'Not if you don't want this thing run up a tree.'

'It's climbed damned near everything else.'

Twig went below, avoiding the passenger deck and dropping on down to the freight and boiler deck, nearly at water level, where the boat's galley was located. He knew Chub Hawks, the cook, from seeing him around Wenatchee City, and Hawks piled a big breakfast in front of him. Hunger, gathering in Twig since the previous noon, came to focus instantly. Joe Blanco, the engineer and fireman, drifted in for coffee, and there were three deckhands keeping out of sight of the passengers while the boat was under way.

They were all tough river hands and a crew that made Twig think of his erstwhile trail riders. They were curious as to what Oak Tully's son was doing riding a stern-wheeler, but none of them asked questions. Twig knew they were as loyal to Abner as his men had been to him. Considering what might lie ahead, that made Abner's friendship and help all the more valuable.

Twig took on some extra coffee, smoking and talking with them, then he went back up to the pilothouse. By then he was getting located again in a country he had once thought he knew from end to end. Off through the chilly distance to the east lay

Badger Mountain. Pine Canyon Landing wasn't far ahead, Abner told him, and beyond that were the Entiat rapids, over which the steamer would have to be lined.

Abner had been joking about turning the wheel over to him, for while it didn't keep him silent it kept him busy. The stretch of river from there to Brown's Landing was easily the wildest steamboat water in the West. The boats had had to be built specially for it, stout of frame and powerful of engines. The shipwrights had done their job. Judah had made his line the main connection between the Wenatchee Bend country and the outside world. He would keep it that way until, if ever, a railroad came through that particular part of the Columbia desert.

Twig found every minute of the long hours of the run exciting. Everything that wasn't water seemed to be solid rock. Sometimes there were quiet stretches but far more of them were roaring demons given to unexpected shoals and snags and chutes so swift the panting little *Chief* seemed to have all it could handle to stand still. More than once a line had to be fixed to a ringbolt embedded in the shore rock so the boat could reel itself upstream. In early afternoon they met the *Arrow* going down, and Twig believed what Abner said about Zeke's problems being more of holding back than making headway.

Then Abner asked a strange question, saying, 'Why don't you learn the trade and really get out of the cattle business?'

'Me? How come?'

'Well, Judah's been talkin' about sending down the river for another pilot so me and Zeke could get a little time off once in a while. Maybe you could talk him into letting me train you, instead.'

Leave the cattle game permanently? Twig had never thought of that, but it felt good to be free to do it if he wanted.

It was all but dark when the *Chief* tied up at the end of its run. Some of its passengers had got off at landings along the way. Most of them, however, had even farther to go and, after spending the night in Judah's hotel, would take the morning stage for the mining camps up the Okanogan. Twig felt that he should pay for his passage and helped unload the freight and express.

Beyond an exchange of greetings, he didn't see Judah until after the landing had absorbed the new arrivals and again settled down. Then Judah took him into the family quarters at the hotel and gave him a drink and a cigar.

'So what I told you a while back sunk in,' Judah commented.

Twig knew Abner had explained his unprecedented manner of arriving at Brown's Landing. 'It sure did,' he agreed. 'Once I got

91

to thinking along that line, what you said tied in with too many other things not to sink in. And deep.'

'Well, I think I done the right thing,' Judah mused. 'And I think you have, too. I mean in a personal way. Oak forgets he had all the freedom in the world to grow up in. That's what taught him what he knows, made him what he is. It's what every man's got to have to really learn.'

Twig was no longer surprised that all the Browns understood what his situation had been because of the accident of being born the son of a man like Oak Tully. Maybe the men had liked his old-time friendship with Melissa, and this had caused them to notice and think about him more than he had guessed. He said, 'I'm glad you think so, but I'm not exactly a free man, even yet. I'm sure you're right about Dill Humminger. Are you ready to tell me what you know about him?'

Judah pulled on his cigar and nodded his head. 'You know Cultus Joe?'

'By sight.'

'Well, a while back I caught him and a fair-sized cut of fat OT beef crossing the corner of the Indian reservation. At first I thought he was stealin' it himself. Stopped him, but he had a bill of sale made out to a butcher in Ruby and signed by Humminger. His sneakin' around that way, when he had a bill of sale smelled mighty fishy. I'd have bet my bottom dollar the proceeds never did and never would reach Oak.' Judah leaned forward to knock ash from his cigar into the draft of the stove. 'I could have told Oak. And he might have waited to see if Humminger reported such a sale and when he didn't he might have asked him about it. Humminger would say I'd been seein' things, and who would Oak believe?'

'Dill,' Twig agreed. 'No, I've got to get the real goods on him, and I'm going up to Ruby. Do you remember the name of that butcher?'

'Dan Tyler. He's opened shops in several camps up there, and his reputation hasn't been good from the start. But what do you expect to find?'

'Well,' Twig admitted. 'Not live steers if he knew what he was buyin', and it looks like he did. But you can't rush hides into miners' bellies and I might find a green one around carrying OT's brand. That'd prove it. I've done every lick of the trail work for the past year, and I haven't taken a head to Ruby the past year. Especially to Dan Tyler. The way they were delivered convinces me, at least, he got 'em at a big discount from Dill. And Dill still turned a neat profit.'

'Well, you've got to start somewhere,' Judah reflected, 'but that kind of operator covers up fast. I'll lend you a horse.'

'I better take the stage,' Twig said, shaking his head. 'I'm supposed to be looking for a new job or some new line of work, and that's how I'll play it up there.'

'I sure wish you luck. But if you don't have it, come back and see me. I might have an idea or two of my own.'

'I sure will,' Twig said. 'And thanks, Judah. You've stuck your neck way out for me.'

'Not nearly as far as you're stickin' yours,' Judah replied. 'Don't forget that Humminger could settle everything by getting you dropped out of the picture. He's got men workin' for him as bad or worse than he is, and if you make it too hot for 'em, they might try.'

'I know that.'

'You got a gun?' Twig shook his head. 'Well, from here on you're gonna have one, and where you can get it quick. To this point, my conscience don't bother me. But it sure would if I caused something to happen to you.'

Considering what he knew now, Twig realized that Judah wasn't stretching the danger. The beef delivery Cultus Joe had made was probably one of many, for there were mining camps and dishonest butchers all over the country. That meant a lot of crooked money had gone into greedy pockets, money that was Oak's and, in the long run, his, too. If he had any doubts about the step he had taken, there wasn't a trace of them left.

He slept as soundly that night as he had slept on the *Chief,* feeling free and on his own and pitted against a challenge as big as any Oak had ever faced. If he won out, Oak would know about it, and Lorna would. If he lost, there was one thing nobody could take away from him – his knowledge that he could be a man in his own right.

Judah rapped on his door sometime before daylight to get him ready to leave on the northbound stage. He brought along a gun and belt. The six-gun was a Colt .44 with well-worn grips, but it was in good condition. He also brought a cowhide valise in which was shaving gear, underwear and socks, and a couple of clean shirts from the store.

'For looks,' Judah said. 'Even if you never change clothes or shave. A man don't go lookin' for new prospects with nothin' but his shirt and pants. How are you fixed for money?'

'Well, I come off without drawin' my pay,' Twig said.

'But I happened to have some cash left from my buyin' trip, so I guess that makes it about even.'

He had given up trying to thank any of the Browns for their favors. He and Judah shook hands, for Judah would be busy from then until after the stage and steamer had left. Twig put the gun rig in the grip then took the bag downstairs, and went into the dining room to get his breakfast. He wasn't exactly champing at the bit, but he was glad to be moving on some kind of a planned course.

CHAPTER SEVEN

It made Dill feel like one of the landmarks to remember that, when he first came to the country, the new railroad town of Ellensburg had been a trading post called Robber's Roost. He had reason to think of himself as a pioneer, for the place had still been called that when Oak found him there and took him on. That had been a fork in the road for Dill. Until the day when he ran into Oak, he had been tempted to have a part in the situation that gave Robber's Roost that name.

At the time the valley of the Kittatas had been ruled by a renegade white man known as Bill Wilson, who somehow had managed to make himself leader of the valley Indians. The nearby Swunk and related camps had been swarming with men then, and stockmen were bringing cattle into the valley itself to fatten on the rich grass. Wilson and his Indian *bandidos* had preyed on them mercilessly for a number of years until, trying to get away with a band of stolen horses, he got himself drowned trying to swim the Snake.

Homeless and wandering, Dill had been

97

on Swunk Prairie then, a boy of fifteen who had learned how to take care of himself. He had run into Wilson, who had taken a shine to him and tried several times to tow him off with him. It had been close, for Dill had been about to throw in with him when Oak hit camp looking for trail hands. He aimed to drive north to the Cariboo, Oak had explained, a gold region so fabulously rich it made the local bars slim pickings. Dill had forgotten Wilson and signed on.

Now the town by the railroad on the valley flat teemed with a new population of cattle-men, dirt farmers, Indians, and Chinese, as well as a more staid element of business and professional people. Dill had arrived there in the mild weather of early December on his first trail job after taking that work back from Twig. The cattle he had brought from the Peshastin ranch, to be shipped out of Puget Sound, were already in the loading pens.

Dill had sent the trail crew, which he knew disliked him, on their way back to the ranch. But he was still in town, intending to cut loose his wolf and not wanting any of Twig's sympathizers around to keep tabs on him. Afterward he would take the train down through the valley of the Yakima and up the Columbia desert. This would put him in minimum time and maximum comfort at Twin Wells, where Sid Lublin would be shipping out the Christmas beef.

On the first evening after the trail crew pulled out, Dill was shining up to a new girl in Frisco Nell's when a man came in who kept him from having his fill from the flesh-pots of the raw town. This was Ned Porter, a gambler from Seattle who was there to take the train for home. A wanderer, Porter had been in the mining camps of the upper Okanogan and had that day ridden directly over the mountain from Wenatchee City.

Porter's question sprang from idle curiosity, but it changed Dill's plans. 'What happened on OT,' he asked, 'to give Twig Tully the itch to go into the mining business?'

Frowning, Dill said guardedly, 'Mining? What do you mean?'

'He was in Ruby when I left,' Porter explained. 'Been there about a week. I never talked to him, but a man said he was talkin' to prospectors like he might buy a claim to develop. How come?'

'Kickin' over the traces,' Dill said with shrug. 'He had a fallin' out with the old man.'

'He crazy? If I stood to come into OT, I'd never stray off the spread. Let alone go huntin' gold.' Porter laughed. 'And my trade's gamblin'.'

Dill managed to pass it off, and the gambler went on about his business. But Porter had taken Dill's mind completely off the roguish eyes and ripe red lips of Frisco Nell's new girl. The last one connected with OT who had seen Twig was Lorna. She said he had simply ridden off into the night. That hadn't worried Dill until now. Twig didn't know anything but cattle work. He had been in and around mining country enough to know what a fickle game mining could be. Maybe it was the lure of the camps themselves that had attracted him, but that didn't sound like Twig. He wasn't a drinker, and his interest in girls was less base than Dill's own.

And why Ruby? The larger, richer, and bawdier camps of the Coeur d'Alene were almost as close to the Wenatchee.

The thought that chilled Dill went beyond Judah Brown's catching Cultus Joe with OT beef bound for Ruby. What if that had reached Oak through Twig, and the row between Oak and Twig was a put-up job? Oak had been about as talkative as a frozen Indian about Twig's leaving and the reason for it. He had simply told Dill to take over the trail work again and then had gone back to Wenatchee City. Dill hadn't seen him since.

Dill plunged out of Frisco Nell's establishment, turned in his room key at the hotel, and carried his saddlebags to the livery barn. Within an hour of his chance conversation with Porter he was on the trail over the

Wenatchee range that the gambler had followed. This was only a saddle and pack trail, but it was shorter than the regular route through the Peshastin country. It would put him in Wenatchee City by daybreak.

His years of work for OT had hardened him to long, lonely hours in the saddle whether by day or night and no matter what the weather. The trail carried him east across the Kittatas and then up into ranges that gained some three thousand feet before they crested and the trail began to drop down. It was cold up there, but he ignored this, and while he was in a hurry he didn't waste the stamina of his horse.

The stars told him daylight was only an hour away when he came down on the Columbia. There was a crossing at that point that had long been used by travelers and cattle. But Dill turned immediately north, pressed by mountains on his left but following easy ground. Just as dawn broke over the bend country he reached his destination. Knowing that Oak was still an early riser, Dill went directly to the Tully house.

Lorna didn't get up as early, and probably at Oak's insistence since she spared herself no pains when it came to taking care of him. So when Dill went in through the back way, he found Oak alone in the kitchen, drinking coffee he had made for himself and smoking a cigar.

Oak seemed in an improved mood, for he smiled and said, 'Well, you must've got up before breakfast.'

'Haven't had it yet,' Dill said. It was warm in the kitchen, so he took off his coat and dropped it on a chair with his hat. Knowing it was permissible to do so, he poured coffee for himself, then sat down near Oak's wheelchair. And then he said, 'I didn't come down from the Peshastin. I rode over the range from Ellensburg last night.'

'You did? What's the rush.'

Dill knew how to put over the idea that he was as unsparing of himself in his own way, as Lorna was in hers. He shrugged in self-disparagement. 'I figured to go over to Crab Creek and see how they're comin' with the Christmas beef. When I got to Rock Island I thought I might as well ride up here first and see you.'

'Any trouble on the Ellensburg drive?' Oak asked.

'Went fine. That leaves the Peshastin pretty well settled for winter.'

'How do you like the new feeders?'

Dill was tactful enough to pass up the chance to be critical of Twig's purchases on the Okanogan. If he found out what he wanted to know, the sharpshooting phase of his life might be over. He said, 'Nice lookin' bunch of steers.' His heart had quickened, for this was the chance he wanted to see for sure how he himself stood. 'By the way. I seen a fellow who just come down from Ruby. He said Twig's there tryin' to get himself a start in the mining business.'

Oak was so openly surprised Dill knew he had nothing to fear about having something put over on him that Oak was in on. Then Oak said with a snort, 'Well, that sounds like him. Easy pickings. Make himself a million dollars overnight and show the old man what he can do if he's given his head.'

'He'll grow up,' Dill said charitably. 'Just give him time.'

'He's had time.'

That was all Dill wanted from Oak, so he was pleased when at that moment Lorna came into the kitchen from the hallway. In her morning freshness of face and dress she was a sight to make a man catch his breath. And she was in such a smiling good humor Dill knew that Twig's departure hadn't upset her anywhere near like it had Oak.

'Hello,' she said cheerily. 'I didn't think Oak was talking to himself, but I had no idea it was you.'

She knew what was gong on in the ranch work, usually, and that he had ridden a far piece to get there. She watched him with an expression that quickened his heart for he had never seen it in her eyes before. She appreciated his limitless loyalty to Oak, which had never shown up so plainly before, and she recognized that it made a bond between them. Dill had always figured himself to be handicapped with her, for Twig was so much younger and much less somber of disposition.

'How are you, Lorna?' he said.

'Fine. And you?'

'For one thing, he's hungry,' Oak said. 'When it comes to that, so am I.'

'When it comes to that, so are all three of us.' Lorna laughed and went over to the big kitchen range. By then Dill felt amply rewarded for his long ride to make sure how he now stood with the two. Oak held nothing against him, so nothing Twig had said had taken root. Lorna wasn't brooding over Twig's leaving, and she must know she could have married him, if she chose, and been fixed for life.

All through the breakfast that was soon on the table Dill kept thinking how pleasant it was to have only the three of them there. By the time he was ready to leave he was fully confident that everything would fall into his lap. That made his trip to Crab Creek all the more important, and as soon as they had finished breakfast he excused himself and left.

It would have been a hard day's ride to the pens at Twin Wells even for a man who had gotten his rest. So Dill went only as far as a deserted Crab Creek winter camp, which he reached in early afternoon. He slept there from early dark to late dawn, and shortly after noon on the day following he reached the shipping operation.

The railroad company had built the pens and chutes in one of the countless coulees of the Columbia desert. The surrounding flats of this one made good holding ground. Out on the white sage range beyond, crews were gathering the winter feeders into bunches and cutting out those ready for sale. As rapidly as the trains took out the loaded cars and switched in empties, more steers were brought into the coulee to be loaded by a crew directly under Sid Lublin.

This was the most profitable single operation OT ran and, watching the work as he rode in, Dill warmed to the thought of the proceeds one day being his through his wife. As he saw it by then Lublin was a more worrisome threat to the prospect than Twig. The returns from the stealing that had gone on so long went into the pockets of Lublin and his intimates as well as into Dill's. Even if it hadn't become so dangerous, Dill no longer cared to share with men for whom he had no further personal use.

Yet he arrived as the range boss, nothing else, and spent the rest of the day watching the loading and making sure the beef lived up to the reputation OT had made for itself with the meat dealers in Portland and the cities on Puget Sound. He checked the tally cards and took hand enough in directing the work to remind Lublin, as well as the others, that he still packed a punch second only to Oak Tully's. The day's freight came by at dusk and took out the loaded cars and left more empties.

It wasn't until that evening, in the chilly open camp, that Dill talked with Lublin confidently. It was the hour after supper when the hands were all stirring around with the last chores of the day. So there was no one at the fire but the ranch foreman and himself.

Bluntly, Dill said, 'Well, Sid. You won't think so little of Judah Brown catching Cultus Joe when you hear what it started.'

Lublin took his eyes off the cigarette he was rolling and looked up, frowning. 'What it started? What do you mean by that?'

'I mean that, this trip, you damned well better listen to what I tell you. Judah sure as hell told Twig about that. And Twig's up in Ruby checking, right this minute.'

'No,' Lublin said, blinking his eyes. 'You're tryin' to twist my tail.'

'If I was gonna twist anything, it'd be your neck. My name was on that bill of sale, and the rest of the thing was in your handwritin'. If Twig gets hold of it and takes it to Oak, you and me are on our way to the pen.'

Lublin was taken aback, but his cocksureness wasn't long in reasserting itself. 'How's he gonna get hold of it?' he retorted. 'You think Tyler's fool enough to hand it over to him?'

'What do you suppose he wanted a bill of sale for, you knothead?' Dill fired back. 'To protect himself. If Twig makes it too hot, Tyler'll flash that thing and claim he had no idea the stuff had been rustled.'

'*If* Twig makes it too hot. What's he got to go on but guesswork? He'll poke around up there, see he's gettin' nowhere fast, and go home.'

'Not home. Him and Oak had a row, and Twig quit his job. He blames me for it. He ain't gonna stop huntin' a way to fix me. So we're gonna keep our noses clean, you hear?'

'Maybe you're right.' Lublin lit the cigarette with an ember, then tossed the glowing stick back in the fire. 'He could've quit his job to throw us off and give him a better chance to dig up somethin'.'

'You're gettin' the idea,' Dill agreed.

'Yeah.' Lublin nodded his head. 'But you ain't got it yet. The hell with your notion of hornin' him out of the herd and keepin' him horned out. You want to have to keep doin' that as long as Oak lives, even after you've married the filly? You want to be scared to make a move for fear he'd be there somewhere just waitin' for you to make it?'

Dill saw in one awful flash that he had laid

it on too thick. He gasped, 'Now, wait a minute!'

'Wait, hell. I'm done with that.'

'We're not gonna–'

'No, we ain't. But I'm gonna. Or I know the man who will.'

CHAPTER EIGHT

The girl's name was Trixie, and her time was Twig's as long as he kept drinks before them on the table in a smoky corner of the Silver Salmon saloon. Lowering her voice to a whisper, Trixie said, 'Twig? You know that fellow at the bar? Beat-up hat and dirty sheepskin?'

Twig lifted his gaze and let it drift casually over the crowded card tables to the less jammed bar beyond. The man Trixie described was easy to pick out, a highcoupled, lath-like figure. His frayed shiny levis spelled close acquaintance with a saddle. That might have caught Trixie's eye and drawn out her question, for Twig was the only other man there not dressed like the miners thronging in the big room.

'Not to know of,' he said. 'Why?'

'He keeps watching you in the mirror.'

'Me? It's you, if anybody.'

She grimaced. 'I hope not, with an expression like that.'

The man had stopped looking at them, if he had actually been doing that. In a moment he put down his shot glass, dropped a coin on the bar, and walked out. The side view dinged a memory in Twig, but it was too faint to explain itself.

'What was wrong with his expression?' he asked.

'I dunno. Just seemed to be taking your measure. It made me feel creepy.'

'Maybe he was figurin' his chances of taking you away from me.'

'You wouldn't catch me dead with a shytepoke like that.'

Twig grinned at her. She had been in as many cow towns as mining camps, he had gathered. He wondered if she knew more about the fellow than she let on. He knew it would do no good to pump her. She had learned the line between saying enough and too much. Even so, she had helped him in several ways.

A cute trick, Trixie drew a lot of patrons to the Silver Salmon, where it was her business to induce them to empty their pockets buying drinks. She was an expert and at first he thought she was the one who had made their hookup, not himself in hopes of digging something out of her wise little head. It hadn't been easy, although he had taken to monopolizing her for an hour or two each evening. Yet once she began to trust him, she had answered some questions, guardedly at first and then more willingly.

He knew the reason for her caution. Camps like Ruby swarmed with investigators, checking into the real value of some touted ledge or the worth of mining stock being boomed for sale. But his questions usually dealt with the region's meat supply, and one night Trixie had said, 'Hey. You a range detective?'

That had told him. Trixie had been around cow country, too, and by then he thought he could confide in her. So he said candidly, 'No, but you're gettin' warm. I'm trailin' some missing steers. The brand was OT.'

The brow knit under the dangling strands of light hair. 'OT? The big outfit down in the basin?'

'That's right.'

'You work for it?'

'Did.'

'And don't now?'

'Nope.'

'Then how come you care whether it's short any steers?'

'Well, the outfit happens to belong to my dad.'

She looked at him in surprise. 'And I thought you were a drifting cowpoke trying to get rid of his money till you started to ask so many questions. Well, I can't help you. I grew up on a ranch myself, and I notice steers when I see 'em. OT's I'd have noticed in particular because that brand's known even down where I come from. And I never did.'

He hadn't expected her to hand him what he wanted, just like that. But nobody knew more about what went on in a mining area than a popular girl in a popular saloon, and she answered questions he would have spent days trying to answer for himself. As Judah had said, Dan Tyler had a smelly reputation. It was said that when he couldn't buy rustled beef cheaply enough he went out and rustled it himself. Trixie knew his physical set up, and this helped Twig to pay secret visits to the ranches around Ruby and Conconully that held stuff for Tyler while it waited to be butchered for his shops.

It had been slow work, for he had to be careful, and there were pestiferous interruptions. The story he told when he had to explain himself was that he was looking for a prospect to buy and develop. So all kinds of people had tried to sell him one, and he had been obliged to listen to them and sometimes actually look at some dusty hole in the ground somebody hoped to pass off on him. And he had found nothing connected with his real purpose of anymore value.

The answer was that the OT beef Tyler had received had all been slaughtered and the hides so well hidden, perhaps at the bottom of some old shaft, although he had risked his neck investigating some of these, too, that there wasn't a trace of one to be found.

So on the evening when Trixie pointed out the tall man with the dirty sheepskin coat and battered hat, Twig had been on the point of telling her he was licked and would pull out the next day. But before he said anything, he was bothered again by the impression that the man wasn't a total stranger. Besides, the fellow's interest had worried Trixie, who wasn't a girl to see a snake behind every blade of grass. Seemed to be taking your measure she had said. And she had been quiet ever since.

Leaning forward, Twig said quietly, 'Look. That bean pole boogered you. You think I stirred up something, somewhere, without knowin' it?'

'You could have,' Trixie said, without lifting her eyes. 'I never seen him before, but he sure made a study of you. And he had the look.' She glanced up then and tried to smile. 'Don't let me spook you. I get moody sometimes and think the world's coming to an end for me or somebody I like. Just the same – well, in your place, I wouldn't drink anymore tonight.'

Twig was far from drunk and knew that the liquor Trixie had consumed was mostly creek water. But he wanted to be alone to think about this and agreed and told her good night. Coming onto the quarter-mile-long street of log buildings, he checked in all directions but saw nothing of the tall man.

Trixie's reaction had left him with conflicting feelings. The first was dread, for he had never had a man on his trail. Yet it was exciting to think that somewhere in his poking around he had come closer to the mark than he had known. The puzzler was just where that had been.

The nearly treeless slopes above the creek valley had been left carpeted by the snow that had brought his own life to a climax, and the outdoor night was cold. This had emptied the streets so that he met no one while he walked down to the hotel where he had taken a room. But there in the cramped lobby a man was waiting for him, although he wasn't the tall man.

This one was a miner beyond question, and he looked cold, hungry, and threadbare. *Another one of those,* Twig thought impatiently when the man shot to his feet and came forward, intercepting him at the foot of the stairs.

'Hold up a minute, mister,' the man said. 'You this Tully I hear's lookin' for a prospects.'

Twig knew he had to carry out that troublesome fiction and said, 'Well, I've been lookin' around. But I'm pullin' out in the morning.'

'Oh no. Not till you've seen what I got to show you. It's a dandy, mister. I ain't showed it to a soul, so far.'

114

'Where's it located?'

'Two – three hours ride from here. I'll show you how to get there. The name's Pike. We can ride out to my camp tonight, and you can see for yourself in the mornin', and if you don't like it you can light your shuck. But you'll like it. Any man in his right mind would. Come on. My horse is just down the street, and we'll get yours.'

The urgency could have sprung from enthusiasm, but a warning sounded in Twig's mind. Suspicious for the first time, he said, 'Why not in the morning?'

'I'd as leave nobody seen us leave camp.'

There was a way to find out how genuine this was. Twig said coldly, 'Well, I eat breakfast at the Gem. Meet me there in the mornin' and I'll say which way I'm going.'

'I got a real comfortable camp–'

'Meet me in the morning, Pike, or forget it.'

Pike was clearly disconcerted, but after a moment he managed to grin. 'No harm sleepin' on it, I reckon. I'll catch you in the mornin'.'

Twig went on up the stairs. Since his room was nearly as cold as the outdoors, he undressed and went to bed. The skinny man and then Pike, he reflected, vague identities who had disturbed him more than anyone he had met up with on Salmon Creek so far. Maybe what Trixie had called her melancholy moodiness had been responsible for his own feeling in both cases. The miner seemed to be the real goods, as far as calling went. Yet he could have been hired to tow him out of camp and surely hadn't liked having to wait overnight to do it.

Twig couldn't convince himself that he was manufacturing bugaboos. Before he fell asleep he had decided it was worth the time and risk to find out for sure. Forewarned was forearmed, and if there was a connection between Pike and the thin man, things might begin at last to unravel.

Pike wasn't waiting for him outside the Gem restaurant the next morning, nor was he inside. Twig went in and ate his breakfast convinced that he had had bait dangled in front of him that he had been smart to spurn. Yet he came out of the restaurant to see Pike leaning against a hitching rack and smoking a wreck of a pipe.

'Well, how about it, Tully?' he asked eagerly. 'You ready to go get rich?'

'All right,' Twig said. 'Let's have a look at this marvel.'

'You won't be sorry, man. You sure won't be sorry.' Twig had been renting a horse at the livery, and that was where Pike said he had put up his own. The hotel was across the street from the team, so while he waited for a horse to be saddled, Twig went over and got the gun Judah had loaned him, which had been in his valise ever since. He saw Pike's eyes drop to look at it, when he returned to the team, but the miner said nothing. If Pike had a weapon of his own, it was hidden on him somewhere.

In another five minutes they had ridden off the end of the street on a rough road that would take them out through Conconully, up the creek from Ruby. The morning was bitter cold, but the sky was clear. The gulch narrowed and widened and narrowed again. All along the way there were remains of old diggings from the days when there had been placer gold along with the silver.

Pike didn't go as far as the upper camp. At the lower end of a lake formed by a narrows, he turned wordlessly west along the left fork of the creek. This gulch pinched out rapidly, and ahead of them loomed the rise of Old Baldy Mountain. The trail they followed presently was worn but old, and it didn't show signs of much travel.

An hour afterward they reached Pike's claim. It was a genuine quartz workings cut into the hillside at an enormous expense in hard labor. There was a wickiup shelter where the miner lived, and a tailings dump spilling away down the ravine. Pike's excitement began to crack through again, although he was now trying to suppress it. Twig realized he had done the man an injustice he couldn't square, even with himself.

'Well, there she lays,' Pike said expansively. 'God knows how many millions, just waitin' to be dug out.'

'What makes you so sure of that?' Twig asked. 'Can you back it with assay reports?'

'Nope. Didn't need 'em. After the time I've spent lookin' for pay rock I know it when I find it.'

'You sure ought to have had it tested before you got yourself so excited.'

'Them plagued assayers leak like sieves,' Pike said with a dismissing motion of a very callused hand. 'Let one of 'em see a chunk of my ore, and every inch of Old Baldy'd be staked before you could say St Wapniackle.'

Twig started to have second thoughts, for here was another loony prospector so beat up by failures he had finally gotten drunk on dreams. Pike had swung down and was waiting for him to do so, but Twig shook his head.

He said, 'Pike, I can see right now that what you've got here is way out of my reach. I shouldn't have taken your time.'

'Reach? You mean money?'

Twig nodded, hoping he could let the man down without too much of a bump. 'I know you told me what a prospect you've got, but I didn't grasp it. You'll have to find you a man with more money than I'll see the rest of my life.'

'Why–' Pike pulled in a disbelieving

breath, his eyes bewildered. 'Why, the feller told me your old man's corralled most of the money in the country.'

It was Twig's turn to look puzzled. Trixie was the only one he had told of his connection with Oak Tully, and it had surprised her. 'My old man?' he asked.

'Sure. That's Oak Tully, ain't it?'

'Well, yes.'

'And this jigger said he's lookin' for a good minin' investment, and that's what you was up here about.'

'Who was it said that?'

Pike shook his head. 'Never spoke his name. Rode in yesterday sayin' he was huntin' him a claim to buy, himself. When he seen this beauty, he said what you did – it was too steep for him. And then he told me about you. Well, I thought her over and decided it was my chance to cash in finally and headed for Ruby.'

'What did this fellow look like?'

'Well, he hardly looked like he'd have a plugged pickle, himself. Hungry lookin' and shabby as I am. A tall, skinny galoot.'

The muscles between Twig's shoulders had pulled into knots. He didn't have to ask if the man had worn a battered hat and dirty sheepskin coat, he knew. Pike was innocent, but this ride into the empty countryside was anything but. Twig could all but feel sights trained on his back.

He managed to say calmly, 'Sorry to disappoint you, Pike, but he was dead wrong. I don't have a cent to invest for anybody but myself, and that's not the kind of money you're looking for. I'm sorry the two of us led you wrong and wasted your time.'

It was apparent that Pike wanted to waste no more of it on a man of penny-ante means. He shrugged and said, 'Live and learn.'

Twig reached down to shake hands with him. Then, feeling an urge to spur the livery horse, he rode back down the gulch, leaving Pike to dream on.

Twig was in anything but a woolgathering mood himself, for he had formed a clear picture of what he faced. For all their sly secretiveness, characters like Pike were notorious. The thin man, or whoever he worked for, had thought of Pike as a means of getting the victim out of camp without its being connected with them in any way. They knew that, having passed himself off a would-be investor, Twig would have found it awkward to refuse to look at the prospect. Since the thin man was a stranger in camp, he must have been brought in by Dan Tyler. That had taken time and was why he had beaten the bushes so long before he stirred up anything.

CHAPTER NINE

It was the first time in his life Twig had been forced into a ride not knowing at what moment he would come under a dry-gulcher's sights. It made him feel cold and queasy and ready to grab his gun every time something stirred in the sagebrush covering the floor of the gulch and climbing the rocky slopes. Stranger though he was in the country, he would have gambled on finding his way back to Ruby along another route. But at present there was no way to get out of the depression because of cutbanks and high faces of rock.

The shot and what followed came too fast for him to think of anything but trying to save himself. He didn't even know if the crash of sound, and the slug that swept away his hat, came from left or right. It was the livery horse, indolent to that moment but all at once a bolt of lightning that inspired him to tumble to the ground as if he had been hit along with the hat. The animal reared and, when it came down, Twig rocked drunkenly and let himself roll to the right. He slid on to the ground, somehow freeing his feet from the stirrups just as the horse bolted forward and then lined out a gallop.

The bushwhacker apparently thought that his one shot had done the job and he didn't try to drop the horse. He didn't shoot again at all immediately. Realizing he had gained a degree of protection by making himself a less visible target, Twig pressed to the ground. His heart drummed like the hooves of the receding horse. If he didn't panic, he would get a chance of his own, for the man would have to make sure of results and to do that would have to expose himself.

His hat rolled too far off to reach, but Twig saw that it had sailed forward and off to his right. So the shot had come from the left, and the dry-gulcher had let him ride a little past before he laid it in. Twig moved himself by cautious inches until he had a better view of the spot from which it might have come. There were plenty of rocks and sage bushes up there, but nothing else was in evidence.

He was calm again, set on the thing before him and nothing else. The hired gunman had vision troubles of his own. Now the odds were on his side, for there had to be a point where the gunman would be required to take a longer chance than he had taken so far. It seemed a long while in coming, but Twig waited with cool patience. Then he heard the sound of a dislodged rock rolling down the slope. He felt his heart quicken, but he didn't move a muscle and his nerves stayed steady.

And then he saw the top of a hat edge out at the side of a rock. It was the oldest of tricks but it often worked on jittery nerves. Twig didn't fall for it, but his mouth pulled into a tighter line. The hat slowly moved out of sight, but it had shown him precisely where his man was. That increased the odds a little more. Then the gunman took his chance and lifted his head above the rock. It was who Twig had expected it to be. Twig let the man's shoulders appear, and then he sent a shot whipping up the slope.

The crash of his gun drowned any sound from up there. But he didn't think the man had fired again, and now there was nothing but empty air above the rock. The thin man knew his intended victim was still alive and full of fight, so Twig used the moment to shove up and run forward, climbing a little. This brought him into the slope cover himself, and he drew his first full breath.

Although his ears ached from straining, he heard nothing but the native sounds of the countryside. It was folly to suppose the hired killer had stayed put, but impatience drove Twig in careful advances toward his last known position. All at once he halted, arrested by something occurring within himself. In those few breaths before he shot he had had his first full-face view of the man. Recalling the face now, he knew why the fellow had seemed vaguely familiar when Trixie pointed him out in a concern now proven well founded. The slashing scar across the end of the mouth cinched it.

Stringer Hames.

This meant that Ruby's crooked meat dealer might have nothing to do with it at all. Stringer wasn't the kind of gunslinger Tyler could have imported. Hames didn't hire out but killed to serve his own purposes or those of his cronies. And he had several cronies in the tough-bitten crews Dill had got together on the ranches on the east side.

Aware that he was up against more than getting back to Ruby alive, Twig crept grimly on toward his objective. Nothing challenged him, for there was no one behind the rock any longer. But there were dark blotches that made a dribbled trail along the slope. Stringer wasn't one to quail because he had spilled a little blood. The one slug must have caught him in the gun arm or shoulder. He was no two-gun marvel, and he was too cagey to gamble his life against long odds.

Yet there was a chance that Stringer would try to decoy him into another setup where his chances would be better. So Twig cut around in a half circle until he came to the top of the ridge. It was more open up there, and he soon found that he need not have worried. Hoof stampings showed where Stringer had left his horse, and the horse was gone. Its rider had bled profusely all the way to it.

Reaction came while Twig was going down the slope, and by the time he reached the bottom his knees were weak and wobbly. He rolled and smoked a cigarette, trying not to believe that Dill could actually have put a killer on his trail. Then he went on down the gulch, following the easily seen tracks of his fleeing horse. As he hoped, the animal had slowed down once away from where it had been frightened. Finally it had stopped to try to graze on the thin crowns of bunch-grass in spite of the bit in its mouth. Twig caught it easily, mounted, and headed for Ruby in a deeper state of perplexity than when he arrived there coming up from Brown's Landing.

One thing was clear. There was no point in staying in Ruby any longer. What he had stirred up pertained to something vaster and grimmer than Tyler and that one cut of stolen OT beef steers. He wanted to leave at once, but he had arrived by stage and would have to go the same way, and that meant laying over until the next morning.

He put in the afternoon in his hotel room, picking at his problems and solving none of them. He had little to do to get ready beyond putting his shaving gear and a few soiled clothes in the valise. He had no intention of reporting his experience to the camp marshal. What had brought Stringer there, and what had happened to him after he fled the scene of the ambush, were things Twig meant to determine himself. And it would be better not to tell Trixie how right she had been in her hunch. The less a girl in her position knew about things like that the better off she was.

But he dropped in at the Silver Salmon that evening to tell her so long since she had been friendly and, in her way, accommodating. He knew it wouldn't bother her. Girls of her kind couldn't afford serious attachments in the weird compulsive quest that took them wherever there were lonely men and loose dollars.

All Trixie said was, 'Oh? Well, *adios*. Maybe our trails'll cross somewhere again.'

'I hope so,' Twig said.

He really meant it, for Trixie's trail after Ruby was as unpredictable as his own. Possibly she would meet some man who would sweep her off her feet and persuade her to marry him. It often happened, and girls of her background could make fine wives and mothers. Just as often they kept following the will-o-the-wisp and, when their youth and looks were gone, wound up in cribs. Because he had really liked her, Twig didn't let himself think about it too long.

It was nearly ten o'clock the next morning when the mud wagon from Ruby brought its load of miscellaneous humanity, mail, and express out of the Salmon Creek gulch and made a rest stop at Pogue's Landing on the Okanogan River. It had been in that vicinity that Twig had made up the fateful herd of winter feeders for OT. This had given him a slight acquaintance with the men who operated the general store, the ferry, blacksmith shop, and saloon.

After the crowding hills it seemed a desert town because of the sage flat on which it stood, shaded only by the trees along the river. Yet it was a busy place because of the steady traffic, not only to the Salmon River district but to camps on up the river. In the high-water months of May and June it even had steamboat service, for then Judah extended the runs of the *Chief* and *Arrow* to that point, competing with the packers and teamsters.

While the stage changed horses and the passengers stretched their legs, Twig sought out the blacksmith, whose yawning doors let him see about everything that happened. The man had never heard of Stringer Hames yet reported that a long-coupled galoot in a battered hat and dirty coat had indeed ridden by in something of a rush the day before. There hadn't appeared to be anything wrong with him, but Twig knew that didn't rule out a bandaged arm or shoulder under the sheepskin coat.

It took several more hours for the stage to run down the river valley to Brown's Landing. The scene at the lower landing was unchanged from what it had been when Twig left there except that it looked even more desolate in the gloomy, late-December day. Judah was too busy with the new arrivals to give him his time, just then, but the *Arrow* was tied up at the wharf boat much earlier than it should have arrived. So Twig went down there to see why this was.

He hadn't got well acquainted with Zeke, but he and Abner were as alike as two peas out of one pod. The trouble was minor, Zeke told him, a little boiler crusting that had forced him to lay up and miss a run. As Twig expected, Zeke knew about his problems with Oak and what he had set out to do. But he asked no questions beyond brief generalities and answered Twig's main question. He was down in Wenatchee City every other night and as far as he heard everything was all right with Oak and Lorna.

Zeke understood why Twig felt this concern with a little extra keenness. Twig hadn't had time to think of it previously but during the dull stage ride it had come to him that Christmas was near. It would be the first one he had spent away from Oak, and from Lorna the last couple of years.

'Look,' Zeke said gently. 'Can't you bury the hatchet with your dad and still do what you have to?'

'No,' Twig said. 'If Oak and me ever shake hands again, he'll have to hold his out the same time I hold out mine.'

'Guess I know how you feel.' Zeke nodded his shaggy head. 'Me and Abner were plumb lucky in our pap. Judah never done nothin' but run stores and hotels in his grown life, and he figured on us boys followin' suit. Yet he never said a word when we wanted to go down the river to work on the boats.' Zeke grinned. 'The old fox let us learn the trade, then snaked us back home by starting his own river line.'

It wasn't until after super that Twig got a chance to give Judah an account of his failure in the Salmon Creek district and of his nearly fatal brush with Stringer Hames. Since Judah had been the first to point out that one sneak shot could settle everything in Dill's favor, he wasn't surprised.

'So what're you gonna do next?' he said, when Twig had finished.

'Go over into the Coeur d'Alene. Hames hangs out there a lot. If he's mixed up in the rustling, those camps are even a bigger market than Salmon Creek. I might dig up somethin' there.'

'Dunno about that,' Judah shook his head. 'Don't forget that a man on a rim with a rifle has got a stacked deck. Hames'll figure you might have recognized him. If you showed up in his own stomping grounds, he wouldn't give you even a chance to see him the next time.'

'I've got to run that risk, Judah. I've got to get to the bottom of it.'

'I know that. But maybe you're going at it wrong, even with no Stringer Hames to consider. Provin' past guilt's mighty dubious, and it sure takes time. Why not put in the same time tryin' to catch 'em red-handed? That'd give you somethin' solid and nailed down.'

'It would,' Twig agreed, 'if they weren't too foxy to do anything I could catch 'em at.'

'They're a greedy bunch,' Judah said stubbornly. 'Men of that cut always are. Lull 'em into thinkin' they were wrong about why you went to Ruby.'

'How can I do that?'

'It stands to reason you've got to line up new work, and you did look at prospects up there. Besides, there was the girl you mentioned. Enough in herself to make a young buck hang around a while. Let Humminger and his cronies get to thinkin' that was all straight goods, and they'll go back to dippin' their fingers in the till.'

Twig cut him a look of wary amusement. 'You got a new line of work in mind, Judah?'

'Well, I have. And I'm the only one who could give you one where you could still keep tabs on OT's east side. Abner said he told you I might hire a new pilot, and how he suggested trainin' a man instead.'

'Such as me.'

'That's right. How does it strike you?'

'Well, fine, but I couldn't do it. I don't think I want to quit the cattle business except temporarily. So you'd waste time trainin' me and still be without your pilot when I get this other thing settled.'

Judah nodded with a gentle smile. 'Wouldn't it be better if you went back to the cattle business and OT and Oak Tully knowing you'd had a choice?'

'It would, and it's mighty white of you, but–'

'The relief pilot? Who knows? If the river gets in your blood like it did in my boys' I might have him for keeps.'

'If you want to gamble on that,' Twig said, grinning, 'I'm game.'

'And you can take all the time you want for your undercover work, and me and the boys will cooperate. You can go down in the mornin' with Abner, and the best way for you to get word of your plans is to tell 'em to Lorna Milne.'

Twig found himself getting excited. It was a smarter idea than he would have thought of himself and extremely generous. As Abner's missing a run to bring hay to his steers had been. As Melissa's prompting when she had thought so poorly of him. The

Brown family would do to ride the river with, he thought, and he was going to do that literally.

Somebody called Judah outside, and Twig went down to the wharf boat where by then both steamers were docked. Zeke and Abner were chewing the rag in the master's cabin of the *Chief*. They weren't surprised to hear of Judah's offer and were pleased that Twig had accepted it.

'Might as well tote your gear ashore,' Abner said heartily. 'The only reason us boys sleep in is to give Melissa company. Me, I like the way the river rocks a man to sleep.'

'You're gonna need a boat cap,' Zeke said, looking him over. 'Can't waste your time grabbin' for your hat.'

'And them ridin' heels,' Abner said. 'You wouldn't be very surefooted in them. Let's go up to the store and get you rigged out like a man ought to be.'

Twig grinned at them, knowing a river man was as vain of his garb as a cowhand. Yet neither kind of clothing was chosen because it was picturesque but because it made sense. But the thing that pleased him was his feeling of being back among friends as warmly loyal as the men in his old trail crew. He had missed those cheerily brash punchers more than he had let himself know.

He was part of the crew the next morning when the *Chief* pushed off for its long and breathtaking run downstream. Abner let him know the first thing that he was to pull his weight, lending a hand wherever one was needed. Twig realized that he had formed a half conscious picture of himself spending his time in the wheelhouse absorbing river lore from Abner. So he worked with the deck crew, in the boiler room, and even helped the cook. But by the time they reached Wenatchee City he realized Abner wasn't just trying to get his money's worth. This close identification with the work side of river transportation had washed out his half-heartedness about it. At the end of the first day he felt like he was really working on the river and not acting a part to hide his real purpose.

He had looked forward all the way down to seeing Lorna that evening. Yet by the time he was free to go ashore in Wenatchee City, this had become diluted by dread. There was hardly a chance that he could catch her at the house with Oak gone handily off somewhere. Twig doubted that, at this sentimental time of the year, he could see them both and still stick to his purpose. And he felt unnatural and conspicuous walking down the familiar street in low-heeled shoes rather than riding boots and with a blue cap on his head. But he had refused to change.

This was the garb he belonged in at present and maybe for a long time to come.

When he had gone along the side street far enough to see Oak's house he felt like hauling around and going back to the boat. Yet there was the practical need to get word through Lorna to Dill of what he was doing. He went on only to hesitate on the porch, wondering if he should knock on the door. The house hadn't been forbidden to him, and he hadn't been disowned yet. He opened the door and stepped into the hallway. And there they both were, Oak and Lorna, staring at him in surprise from the sitting room.

Twig tried to smile, but his cheeks were too wooden to shape one up with. Remembering the cap, he pulled it off his head and went on toward them. Lorna had some kind of needlework in her hands that she put down in her lap. She had her hair done in a new way, combed back and with the ends in long curls.

'Well,' Oak said finally, his eyes raking Twig from feet to head, 'what're you got up as? The bullhorn blower in the band?'

Twig looked down at the cap in his hand, then met Oak's eyes, and held them steadily. Oak's didn't soften to imply that he had made a joke. He had meant it for cutting ridicule. Twig ignored the thrust and managed to say without heat, 'Thought you might want to know where I am, Oak. I've

134

gone to work on the *Chief* for Judah Brown.'

'Last I heard you were makin' a million dollars up in Ruby.'

'Word gets around fast. Who told you that?'

'I heard. And now you're gonna make yourself a transportation king.'

'No. But I'm going to learn the business.'

'I reckon that'll take you all of two weeks.

'I expect it'll take me years.'

'You–?' It had sunk into Oak finally. His face was turning red. 'You mean to say you'd rather work on a steamboat than–'

'I don't know. But I sure aim to find out.'

'All right. You told me. Anything else?'

'I guess that's all.'

Twig knew he had been dismissed and looked at Lorna helplessly. Her face was white as flour, and she refused to meet his eyes. He knew what they thought. He had denied Oak's way of life, rejected and spurned and cast it aside. Worse, in their lights, he had come to flaunt the fact by wearing his river clothes. He turned wordlessly and left the house.

CHAPTER TEN

The *Chief* didn't stay nosed to the bank at Pine Canyon long enough for the down-bound passengers to get curious as to why a stop was being made at a place so deserted. Abner held the steamer there only long enough for Twig to toss a bundle ashore, and leap out after it.

Then Abner backed off, heeled around, and made into the upper end of Rocky Reach.

Twig picked up the bundle and moved quickly away from the riverbank. If he could avoid it he didn't want to be seen. Even with the boat passengers being carried swiftly out of sight, he felt uneasily conspicuous in his boat cap and pea jacket. He had got used to this apparel in his three months on the river, but it didn't blend well with the open range country around him.

He couldn't take his next step until night-fall, so he moved over to the edge of a willow clump, sat down, and rolled a cigarette. East of him wheeled an open plateau that mounted in easy stages to break abruptly in the high rimrock of Moses Coulee. Off to the south Badger rose against the clear spring sky. The brood ranch headquarters lay at the eastern foot of this formation, about ten miles distant from where he sat.

This ranch had been the last on his list because its ranges curried only cows, calves, and steers too immature to go to the feeding ranches. Yet in several secret visits to Injun and Crab creeks, where fat threes and fours grazed by the thousands, he had seen nothing out of the way. So while the brood stock didn't seem very likely to attract rustlers, he was as determined to leave no stone unturned to prove to Oak what had been proved to himself by Stringer Hames at Ruby.

About a mile out from where he sat was a dwarfed huddle of buildings he knew to be a settler's setup. A number of newcomers had filed on homestead claims on the plateau, swearing it could be turned into wheat country as productive as the Walla Walla Valley down south. They were on what had always been OT range, and Dill would have run them off if Oak hadn't learned of their presence and given flat orders against molesting them. Not that Oak welcomed them. He figured they would drought out in a couple of seasons and leave voluntarily.

Yet there were plenty of others who didn't think this at all, and the Browns were among them. Even Twig, in his short experience in the transportation game, had come to sense a change in the times he had never felt before and was sure that Oak didn't suspect. On both sides of the Columbia there were more of these homesteaders than he had guessed. They put more sense in Judah Brown's enterprises than had been apparent to him before.

Twig had, for instance, been surprised at the number of landings made by the packets both upbound and down, signaled to the boats by a red flag on the shore. Sometimes there would be a passenger or a whole family waiting to be picked up. More often there would be nothing to be found but a piece of paper snagged on a hook on the makeshift flag pole. This might be a substantial order for provisions. Sometimes it was for medicine, and not infrequently for no more than a tobacco or a spool of thread. However large or small the order, the stuff would be there on the same landing after the next morning's upboard had gone by.

'We like to accommodate 'em,' Abner explained. 'But it ain't all that. One of these times them people will be shipping out wheat and a pile of it. We want it to be us that hauls it and not the wagoners that always push in after somebody else has scared up business.'

'You think it'll be that important?' Twig had asked, surprised.

Abner grinned at him. 'You don't know

138

yet how smart you were to get out of the cattle business. Wheat's not only gonna take over the big bend of the Columbia it'll go up the Wenatchee and the Okanogan and the smaller valleys. Wheat and maybe fruit. This soil and climate will pop both outta the ground overnight. Settlers'll take over the valleys first, then they'll spread over the benches and hills. And there goes OT and all the other big cattle outfits.'

Twig would have scoffed at that a few months earlier. Now he didn't find it hard to believe. It gave him mixed feelings, for it was shaking to think that anything could put an end to OT. Yet it was exciting to think that he might be living and taking part in a time of massive displacement like the days when Oak and a few others had nudged out the Indians and trappers.

'And when that day comes,' he commented, 'you Browns'll be sitting pretty.'

'Only till a railroad's built north of the Northern Pacific, and it's us that gets shoved into the back seat.'

There were other aspects of his new life that Twig had found absorbing for he had set himself to learn as much about it as he could. At the terminals he had worked with the deck crew rousting freight aboard or ashore. At the wood landings he had gone ashore and helped fill the boiler deck prow with cordwood. Underway he had sometimes fired for the engineer and begun to develop considerable respect for steam, not only its power and dangers but the ins and outs of making it and putting it to useful work. Compared to the horsepower he had always known, steam was a giant of infinite capabilities.

The hours he liked best, however, had been those he spent in the wheelhouse with Abner. First there had been the surprise of learning how much Abner could read from the river surface that slipped out of the forward distance, passed, and fell behind the packet. Abner explained patiently and was a far better teacher than Dill had ever wanted to be. Soon Twig had understood why Abner played the wheel so constantly in what at first had seemed like idle restlessness. He began to understand the reason for every detail in the boat's design and for the carefully planned way the freight was loaded.

There were so many tricks to handling the whole correctly that Twig despaired of ever learning them all. And now he wanted to learn them. He had this thing to do for OT, for Oak, and for himself. But afterward he would have a difficult choice to make as to whether he went back to OT or stayed on as Judah's pilot...

He had to wait at the willow thicket an hour before it was dark enough to move away from the river. Then he picked up his bundle and started out, moving swiftly toward the now visible light of the settler's shack. He expected to have his approach contested by one of the fierce dogs settlers liked to keep on their places. But there was no barking as he came closer, and while he walked in he sent a 'Hallo, the house' rolling ahead of him. A rectangle of light appeared in the black shape of the shack. A heavy voice answered.

Twig went on to see that the man waiting in the doorway didn't have much to fear from the ordinary hazards of life. He was big enough to lick two ordinary men and had a shock of yellow hair and a faceful of yellow whiskers. He must have been surprised by a riverman appearing at his door in the night but he didn't turn a hair.

He said mildly but with a shrewd degree of caution, 'Howdy. You lost?'

'Not if you're Link Sands.'

'Then you ain't lost.'

'Good. The name's Tully, and I'm a friend of Abner Brown.'

'So?' Sands nodded his lion's head. 'Abner send you here?'

'That's right.'

'Thought I heard the boat go down quite a bit before dark.'

'It did,' Twig said. 'But I got off and waited for darkness. I didn't want to take a chance on somebody seein' me come here.'

'Don't know who that'd be, except maybe some OT puncher.' Then Sands cut him a look of inquiry. 'Hey. You wouldn't be *that* breed of Tully, would you?'

'It happens I am, but I don't work for OT anymore.'

He was welcome, finally. Sands grinned and said, 'Well, now. Come on in.'

Abner had told Twig that Sands was unmarried, but the inside of the shack was clean, neat, and comfortable. Sands had just finished a meal, from the looks of the table. He moved immediately to the stove, but Twig stopped him. 'If you're fixing to rustle me some grub, I ate before I left the boat. But if you'll put me up for the night, I'll sure have breakfast with you. And tomorrow, if you'll do me the favor, I'd like the loan of a horse. Abner said you've got some fine saddlers.'

Sands nodded. 'I never fancied forkin' a plow nag when I've got to go somewhere. And you'll get your favor. The Brown boys have done me more of them than I could shake a stick at. Can you use some coffee?'

'Sure can. After the sun went down, it got a little chilly.'

'It's been a pretty good spring, but winter ain't all shook off yet.'

Abner had vouched for Sands's reliability so, while they drank coffee and smoked, Twig told him why he was there. Sands

142

didn't seem surprised at his suspicions of underhanded work on the east-side ranches. Most of his contacts were with the Rock Creek crew. Twig gathered from what he said that while they had obeyed the letter of Oak's order against molesting the settlers they had gone out of their way to be irritating and annoying.

'You don't want a change of management on this side of the river,' he concluded, 'any worse than I do. I'll give you all the help I can.'

With that settled to his satisfaction, Twig began to question Sands about himself, which automatically included wheat. He had come into the big bend from the Walla Walla, Sands said. They had pioneered wheat there, as Twig knew, and now it was a booming business and land there was scarce. 'Folks used to think,' Sands said, 'that the number of farms you could have in a country was limited to the number of valleys. Particularly in a country as hot and dry as Washington and Oregon are on this side of the mountains. But I expect you know about Doc Baker and how he turned that idea clear around.'

Twig nodded. A crippled man who somehow had found time to practice medicine, run a store, a bank, a cattle ranch, a farm, and finally to build his valley its own rail connection with the Columbia, Baker had only recently died. 'But I never heard,' Twig said, 'just what gave him the idea sagebrush country would be so good for wheat.'

'Just that,' Sands said. 'The sage, itself. It stood higher than a man's head down there, like it does here. They say Doc always had a busy mind. It seemed to him that a soil that'd grow a weed that thrivin' ought to grow somethin' useful instead. Everybody laughed at him, and it took him years to prove how wrong they were.'

'And now it's takin' the country.'

'You admit that? And you a cowman?'

'Ex-cowman,' Twig said with a grin. 'In fact, an ex-cub cowman who's now a cub river pilot.'

He awakened well before daylight, the next morning, to find Sands up ahead of him and cooking breakfast. Before he dressed, Twig opened the bundle he had brought off the boat with him. It contained his sheepskin coat, hat, riding boots, and the gun and belt he was still borrowing from Judah.

Sands grinned at him. 'That *is* a little less noticeable than a seafarin' man forkin' a cayuse in the middle of a desert.'

Twig left as soon as he had eaten breakfast, telling Sands that with luck he'd be back that night to wait over and catch the *Arrow* on its way upstream. The settler wished him luck. He had already saddled a fast-looking steel gelding and brought it to the door. He guaranteed its speed and stamina, and then Twig shook hands with Sands and rode out into the still dark night.

Daylight found him on the coulee rim above Rock Creek headquarters, flattened on the rock and with the gelding left back at a distance. The layout below was large and sprawling for it had grown out of what once had been a cow camp and nothing more. Smoke rose from the cookhouse chimney, and he could see a few of the men moving about at morning chores. He didn't expect to have anything betrayed to him there, but he wanted to see how the men broke up into crews and to follow somebody on the day's rounds. He knew the work well enough to detect any departure from normal.

It took patience. He had been there better than an hour before the men were all out of the cookshack and getting their orders from Trink Neysmith, the brood ranch foreman. Twig had hoped to be lucky enough to catch Dill there, but from the distance he saw no one who even bore a resemblance. And then the men broke up and went to the corral to saddle horses.

He had intended to pick somebody to dog at random. What he saw develop changed his mind. Until calf roundup started in May, the cattle here were kept fairly close in. The punchers seldom worked in numbers greater than pairs, and as often as not went about the day's work alone. Yet Twig saw a bunch of four men grouped together. They had saddled themselves horses, and now they were putting packsaddles on more. By the time they were done they had a string of six ponies, which they led over to the commissary.

Although the distance made it hard to see, Twig realized presently that the sacks they began to bring out of the commissary and rope to the wooden saddles held stock salt. There was nothing unusual about a salting operation itself, but that was a lot of salt and four men were at least twice the number needed. This was sufficiently intriguing that he kept his eyes glued on them and forgot the others.

In another fifteen minutes the foursome rode up the coulee, which terminated so near at hand he knew they would soon climb the trail to his level. Pulling back, Twig returned to his horse, mounted it, and rode over to where he could hide himself in a rock nest and yet watch the top of the trail from the coulee bottom. He was still too far away to make out more than their shapes when, in another twenty minutes, the first rider came over, followed by the pack string and then the other punchers. He couldn't tell which ones of the Rock Creek crew they were.

146

They headed off to the northeast along the plateau above Moses Coulee. Twig let them go until there was hardly more than their dust to help him keep track of them. Once the pack animals were settled into line, all the riders moved ahead to breathe cleaner air. When he could no longer see mounted horses, Twig closed the gap a trifle. He could tell that they had a definite destination in mind and that it was quite a ways off from their steady progress northward.

The day grew warmer, and after a while Twig stopped to take off his coat and tie it behind the seat of the saddle. Before mounting again he took time to roll a cigarette, and it was only because of this that he noticed something that kept him from riding into a ticklish situation. Off to the southwest a rider was coming across the open ground at an easy lope. He was far away as yet and seemed to be cutting an angle too sharp to be trying to catch up with the party ahead. Twig wondered if he had been spotted, and decided that he hadn't so far. Moving slowly, he led the horse to the right and toward a crop of rock. His movement had no effect on the lone rider. But Twig knew he dared not emerge and go on with his dogging until he knew what the newcomer would do.

He waited there some twenty minutes watching the new man cut indifferently across the sign left by the packers and go on. That suggested that he was some outsider making eastward and cutting cross-country to save miles. There was a rim break off to the east that would let him cross Moses Coulee. When the rock in that direction had swallowed him, Twig mounted again. By then there was no sign of the packers but their tracks on the dry, sandy ground. That was enough as long as he could see far enough ahead to make sure he didn't stumble into what could be grim trouble. He had only to remember Stringer Hames to curb his recklessness.

At the end of another hour he had followed the sign into a wide band of scabland dividing the Rock and Injun Creek ranges. The roughs were an ancient glacial moraine marked by naked rims and yawning canyons. While there were grassy coulees within them, the cattle were kept away because there were too many chances for them to be hurt. Even the riders stayed out of the scabs except when they had to go in after strays.

Twig reined in his horse, deflated by the suspicion that he had led himself on a long wild goose chase. The only thing that made sense was that the pack string was carrying a load of salt to Injun Creek. One man could have handled that, but the others could be along to help in some perfectly legitimate work at the feeder ranch.

In the next breath he knew this was dead wrong and that he was in for instant trouble if he didn't move fast. Due ahead and coming along the horse tracks he had followed so long, a packhorse appeared out of a rock cleft. Twig knew he hadn't got ahead of them; they were coming back. He took this in with a sweeping glance, whirled his horse and sent it leaping toward a bushy cul-de-sac off to the left. It seemed minutes before he gained cover but couldn't have been more than a few seconds. Swinging down he moved to the head of the horse to keep it quiet while the pack string went by. He could only hope that the men with it didn't notice his tracks leading off.

The horses had all emerged by then, and their wooden saddles were empty. The animals trudged down the line of tracks they had themselves made a while before, as if they had been turned loose to return to Rock Creek by themselves. But a mounted man came out of the cleft behind their dust, just one. He wasn't watching the ground, and he didn't look Twig's way when he passed. If he was a Rock Creek puncher, he had been hired too recently for Twig to recognise him.

Twig stayed where he was, his heart still going fast. The salt had been unloaded in the scabs, and the other three men were still with it. Why? A man didn't have to know much about cattle to make a guess. Steers wouldn't stray far from an area where there was salt to be had. It was an old trick for holding them on a strange range until they had settled and would stay voluntarily.

He knew he was onto what he wanted and could ruin it by bulling blindly into the scabs without knowing what had happened to the other three men. If he was guessing right, there was no rush. They planned to hold beef steers in the scabs, and the only place the stuff could be picked up would be the Injun Creek range on north, there being nothing but brood stock on this side. At present they were only getting set for this. Considering the time of year, it was a good guess that they would wait until after the spring roundup to dispose of the loot. That would give the ranch foremen and Dill a chance to do the necessary doctoring of the books before the steers were even moved off OT.

CHAPTER ELEVEN

Dill had never made up his mind whether Lorna's devotion to Oak sprang from affection, gratitude, or her awareness that Oak was the closest she would ever come to security in her life. Dill no longer had affection for Oak, himself. If gratitude was to be considered, he had discharged his debt from the start and, after all the years, Oak was the one who owed it to him. But Dill could understand the other feeling, if it also was Lorna's. Oak had an aura of the rich and powerful about him that was coveted by those whose earliest memories were of poverty, loneliness, and incessant fear.

But with the coming of spring Dill had finally persuaded Lorna to leave Oak to his own company on a Sunday afternoon, and take a ride with him down along the river toward Rock Island. It was beautiful weather, and once way from the confinement of the house Lorna had lifted to it. Her pleasure had so animated her that Dill had felt the first real stirring of hunger for her as a woman rather than as a means to an end. Now they had come to a shady grove by the river and, before turning back, had dismounted to rest awhile.

While he was stirred by her lively prettiness, Dill still hadn't been able to loosen up. He knew how to be with men without losing command of himself and, in most cases, his command of them. The women in his life had been those easy to meet and have his way with, here, there, and everywhere his work for OT took him. But women of Lorna's cut kept him uneasy, made him feel dull and ungainly. She still affected him that way, even though he had escorted her to several social affairs in Wenatchee city that winter and spring.

He had pressed for this ride thinking the time had come to put in his bid, nothing outright and final but a strong hint of his intentions and hopes and a feeling out of hers. So far he hadn't been able to get his tongue pried loose from the roof of his mouth. Yet Lorna seemed to have an idea something of the sort was coming. He caught her studying him, and she was smiling to herself.

Instead of averting her eyes when he caught her, she said, 'You always been such a jabberbox?'

'Well,' Dill said, and he managed to grin. 'When I want talk there's plenty of men around ready to give me more than I can use. I don't get a chance to look at a pretty girl much. When I do, I keep my trap shut

152

and look.'

'You weren't looking at *me*,' she scoffed. 'Where's the pretty girl? Out there in the river?'

'You know who's the pretty girl. The prettiest ever to come to this country.'

'Prettier than Melissa Brown?' she asked, cocking her head.

Dill looked at her quickly. 'What made you think of her?'

'I've been wondering how much she had to do with Twig doing what he did.'

'You still think about him?' Dill said, his eyes growing dark.

'I can't help it. Oak's not the same anymore. It really hurt him that night Twig came to the house and said he was going on the river with the Browns. I keep wondering what really got into Twig to make him do it.'

'You think it was Melissa?'

'A woman wonders.'

'I know,' Dill said bitterly. 'Oak figured on turning OT over to Twig and you marryin' him, and that would take care of it. But it didn't work out that way. Twig never had it in him.'

'I know,' Lorna confessed with a sigh. 'He didn't.'

'Would you have married him?'

'I don't know. Things hadn't got where I had to know when they just went kerplunk.'

'Why for you?' Dill retorted. 'Oak's still

got you, and he's gonna hold onto you.'

'And he's still got you, Dill,' Lorna said.

'Sometimes I wonder if he knows it.'

'He does. And I'm grateful to you, Dill, for being so loyal to him. I know he is. He's just not a man to show his feelings, but I've got so I can read him. That's how I know how cut up he is about Twig.'

'Twig, Twig,' Dill hooted. 'He's all you think about.'

'Only because I think about Oak. Like you do. We've got a lot in common, Dill. Let's not get in a row about it.'

Her eyes held something that turned his anger into longing, and he said urgently, 'Lorna, can't you see how jealous I am of him? I mean when it comes to you?'

She smiled and put a finger across his lips. The soft, warm touch made him want to grab and crush her to him. 'There's no reason for you to be jealous,' she murmured. 'The man I marry will be a real man.'

'Lorna, would you marry me?'

'Don't ask me yet. I don't know. When I know I'll tell you, one way or the other. Let's go back now. Oak will be wanting his supper.'

Neither of them said much on the ride back to town. But Dill felt better, for he could see to it that Twig never measured up to Lorna's standards, anymore than he had let him measure up to Oak's. All he had left to do was break the hold Sid Lublin had on him. It was a mean hold. Lublin had admitted sending Stringer Hames to Ruby to kill Twig. It wasn't because he loved Twig that Dill had been so relieved to learn Hames had failed and come back wearing a bandaged shoulder himself.

When they reached the house, Lorna asked him to stay and share the cold supper she and Oak always had on Sunday night. Dill accepted with mounting pleasure and sat on the front porch with Oak while they waited for her to set out the food. He managed to get Oak's mind off his secret sorrow by talking about the spring roundup that would soon start and keep them busy into summer. He even jollied Oak and once made him laugh by reminding him of the time one of their punchers tried to prove a polecat was rendered harmless when lifted by the tail.

'I remember that,' Oak said with a chuckle. 'What he didn't figure on was he had to get hold of the tail.'

That got Oak reminiscing, which lasted through supper, and Dill could tell that Lorna was pleased by his efforts. He knew he would have been welcome to spend the evening there, but while part of his mind was feeling fine, another part kept picking worriedly at the problem of Sid Lublin. The man could ruin all this, and roundup was bound to bring things to a head. That was when, in the days when Dill had been a wholehearted part of the scheme, they had juggled the books so there was always unaccountable beef to sell secretly. He knew he had to get it settled with Lublin before then.

So he excused himself, saying he was heading for Crab Creek and would make their west-line camp to spend the night. It always pleased Oak to see that he paid no attention to such things as hours and rest and his own comfort. He had grained his horse in Oak's stable and he tightened the saddle cinch, rode down to the ferry and crossed the river, and then struck off to the southeast.

It was after midnight when he reached the outcamp at Dead Squaw Springs. The two men who had wintered there to keep the cattle out of the potholes and sand dunes were privy to the secret activity on the east side. From their manner, Dill realized that they were aware of the friction that had sprung up between him and Lublin. They were so guarded and evasive that he wondered uneasily if something was afoot, new and unknown to him. This put him in a black mood.

Late that afternoon he arrived at the Crab Creek headquarters. His sense of a coming insurrection was stronger each time he came. This induced him to throw his weight around with the men as well as the ranch foreman, although it grew ever harder to impress them. He kept everything strictly business with Lublin until that night when they were alone in the foreman's room.

Dill didn't think he could get anything out of Lublin without rattling him. So out of a long strained silence he said roughly, 'A little bird told me you're settin' up another caper, Sid. How come you never told me anything about it?'

Lublin cut him a glance so keen Dill knew he was on the right track. The foreman stalled, saying, 'Now, what little bird said that?'

'Never mind.'

'You got a spy planted on me.'

'You don't think I'd trust you after that fool delivery to Dan Tyler. Then sendin' Hames to Ruby to get Twig, on top of that.'

'Twig was there to get the deadwood on us,' Lublin said doggedly. 'You know that as well as I do.'

'Well, it's no thanks to your brains he didn't get it. And don't you try to hand it to him on a platter again.'

Lublin reared back his head, his eyes full of his arrogance. 'He won't catch onto this one, even if him learnin' the steamboat business ain't the real goods. What he'd look for is us tryin' to lift some more beef steers.'

'What else is there to lift?'

For a moment the foreman looked at him with angry eyes. 'So your little bird was a bluff. All right. You had to know sometime, so it might as well be right now. I'm liftin' me a cattle ranch off OT, that's what. Then the hell with you and Oak Tully and that filly you're tryin' so hard to tie up with.'

Dill could hardly believe his ears. 'You gone clean off your rocker?' he gasped.

'Like a fox.' Lublin grinned triumphantly. 'Stringer's picked us up some range in the Idaho panhandle. He can get a lot more by nudgin' out some nesters, and Stringer's mighty handy at that. As soon as we've got enough critters over there, we're goin' partners.'

'So you're gonna steal brood stock.'

'You're damned right I am.'

'It's smart, sure enough. Twig wouldn't think of that. You could clean out the brood ranch with him practically on top of it but barkin' up the wrong tree.'

In mock admiration, Lublin said, 'Well, you caught on.'

'It's smart,' Dill snapped. 'But not smart enough. There's no way on earth I could write off that much stuff. Die-off? Winter kill? Coyotes and wolves? Even rustlers? You chucklehead, Oak knows what that runs to, year after year. Jumpin' it up like you figure on is the best way I can think of to get him to order an audit.'

'Who's problem's that?' Lublin retorted. 'Me and Stringer's gonna have bills of sale for every head of OT's to be found on our spread. What you do to the books don't concern us.'

'It can't be done,' Dill said in cornered fury. 'You try to crowd me that far, and I'll kill you.'

'Try it. I don't mean I could beat you. Maybe not. But I got plenty of friends besides Stringer that wouldn't let you live a day.'

Dill knew that. He had threatened only out of desperation. 'Don't do it, Sid,' he begged. 'It ain't got a chance to come off. Go ahead and steal some more steers. I'll go along with that.'

'You'll go along with this.' Lublin had secured his victory again. He grew more temperate. 'And it won't be as risky as you suppose. I ain't fool enough to think I could move a payin' brood herd into the panhandle all at once. Me and Stringer won't have range enough except as we clear out nesters. So quit shakin'. All we'll take at a time is what you can write off without Oak bein' sure enough somethin' is wrong to dig into it.'

'I see.' Dill passed a hot, dry hand over his eyes. 'You'll bleed me, year after year. And I'll be the one with his neck stuck out for the ax, not you.'

'You've about called the turn. Me and the boys ain't trusted you a bit since you got your wind up over the filly. We sure ain't gonna rely on you takin' care of us if you get her and OT. When I'm ready to go to the panhandle, they'll go with me.'

'How're you workin' it?' Dill asked in a tired, resigned voice.

'The boys're getting ready to cut out the stuff I want and move it into the scabs the other side of Rock Creek. It just won't be on hand to be tallied at roundup. The figures you turn in to Oak will be the real goods. If he wonders why the loss is so high, you can tell him to go out and count it himself.'

'Don't overdo it, damn you. You crowd me into trouble, and I'll spill the whole business.'

'No you wouldn't.' Lublin regarded him with amused eyes. 'You'd have to prove it, or somebody would. And I'd have a pack of witnesses to swear you made a deal with me for brooders and my part was on the level.'

'God damn you,' Dill said helplessly.

Lublin laughed outright. 'You ain't the tall man you figured you were, are you? But it needn't come to trouble. We'll go easy on it because it's too good to spoil. You'll get your gal and then OT, and we'll all be satisfied.'

Dill knew he had to stop this man, and there was no way on earth to do it. False witnesses of his own? There wasn't a man on OT or in the whole country he could call that good a friend. He stared in utter futility at the greed in Lublin's eyes, the drunkenness brought on by the power he had seized.

He'd didn't say another word to Lublin from then until he left early the next morning. And when he rode away, heading on along his rounds of the east side spread, he was feeling more settled. In the sleepless night it had come to him that, if the worst happened, he might be in a position where Oak wouldn't dare to do anything to him personally. Lorna had given him real encouragement during their ride. Afterward she had admitted him to the family circle for the cold supper. He had to persuade her to marry him and soon. Then, somehow, he would find the way to get rid of Lublin. Or, that failing, Oak would have to hurt Lorna to punish him.

CHAPTER TWELVE

The evening was the most pleasant of that spring, shirtsleeve weather with the smell of new growth and early flowers carrying down to the river from the town. The river itself had begun to swell with the spring freshet, and the *Chief* rode a little higher in relation to the bank. Twig had the steamer to himself, that Saturday night, for Abner and the crewmen had drifted ashore. He stood leaning on the rail, smoking a cigarette and wishing there was some way he could see Lorna without the painful experience of running into Oak. There simply was no way he could.

He had just released the stub of the cigarette and watched it drop to the water when a voice called, 'What're you looking so glum about?'

Glancing up, he saw that Melissa had stepped out the door of her private quarters. The summer dress she wore accented the boyish slimness of her body and the girlish curves of her breasts. She had her fair hair combed up on her head, and he gaped a little for it surely made her look pretty. There were a couple of barrel chairs on her deck, and she sat down in one. Instead of answering her, Twig dropped down to the passenger deck and went along the gangplank to the wharf boat. If his joining her pleased her, she did a good job of keeping it to herself. Even so, he sat down in the other chair.

She said, 'Well. You never answered my question.'

'I'm not glum.'

'Oh no? And I know what it is. Saturday night, with all the fellows who've got girls going to see them. So why don't you go and see her? Because of your dad?'

'That's a good reason. Where's your fellow?'

He had been surprised to learn, in recent months, that there were several of them competing for her company. This was the first Saturday night, on which the *Chief* always tied up on this end over Sunday, that she had stayed home by herself.

'Which one do you mean?' she asked.

'Any or all of 'em.'

'I finally managed to discourage them.'

'You're sure picky.'

'Yes.' She nodded her head. 'I am.'

She was looking off at the river, and he watched her from the corner of his eye. He didn't fill the bill with her any better than the fellows she had just mentioned. So she wasn't dangling a loop to see if he'd walk into it. That didn't bother him. He was still

163

mighty grateful for the hay that had got him out of trouble. But as long as Lorna was around, he wouldn't be able to look twice at any other girl. And that seemed to suit Melissa.

'For what comfort it is to *you*,' he heard Melissa saying, 'it wouldn't do you any good even if you could catch Lorna away from your father. Dill Humminger's in town. I saw him this afternoon when I went to the store. He's probably sitting on the porch with her right now.'

'That don't mean he's the one she wants there.'

'The one she wants there,' Melissa said calmly, 'is the one she thinks will win out. Right now it looks like that will be Dill.'

'What did she ever do to you,' Twig demanded, 'to give you such a high opinion?'

'Nothing. To me personally. She hardly knows I'm alive. Because there's nothing she wants that I stand for.'

Twig cut her a look of displeasure. 'Your admiration for the Tully family sure runs out your ears.'

'Well, *you're* doing a little better.' Melissa smiled. 'At least you woke up to the fact that you had a big ring in your nose. You haven't woke up, though, to the even bigger one she'll put there if you come out on top.'

'Women,' Twig said with a snort. 'I guess none of you trust each other.'

'That's not a bad guess. But I'm not sharpening my claws on Lorna Milne. It worries me. You're going to lose even if you win if you don't get both eyes open.'

'You're gettin' your worrying started mighty early, because I sure haven't won out yet.'

Melissa said no more, and he fell to thinking of his strange experience, the week before, over east in the scabs. He hadn't said anything to anybody about it. All he had, so far, was a little evidence and a lot of hunch that luck was about to break his way, finally. Nor had he gone back because it wasn't likely that they would start to run beef steers into the scabs until it could be covered in the confusion of spring roundup. That would be soon, and when the time came he meant to be there continuously until he had got to the bottom of it.

All at once Melissa stood up. 'I think I'll stretch my legs,' she said. 'Want to come along?'

'Why – sure.'

Twig stood up uncertainly. Walking a girl was regarded by the town as the first step toward keeping company. He didn't think Melissa meant it that way, for her manner implied that she didn't care whether he accompanied her or stayed there and mildewed. They crossed the wharf boat gangway and came onto the main street. Settler rigs and cow ponies strung along the street attested to the centralizing influence of a Saturday night.

While Melissa had a short, smooth, girl's step she was quick and he didn't have to slow down for her. A number of townspeople were out, too, taking the air. It bothered him that the women among them kept laying quick looks of interest on him and Melissa. Like he and she were staking a claim to each other and filing the customary public notice. They walked to the south end of town and then went on along the bank of the river. The evening was well along. The air stirring along the river teased little tendrils of Melissa's hair. There was no sane connection, yet this made him think of other girl things, like frailty and tenderness and the promise of sweet surrender, qualities Melissa surely didn't possess.

They thought they had the footpath to themselves and did have until they were nearly out of sight of town. Then all at once they came around a thicket and there, coming toward them and returning to town, were Dill and Lorna. Twig felt like he had run into a patch of nettles, and when he glanced at Melissa she looked as flabbergasted as he was. The same expression was on Lorna's face, while Dill pulled himself straight as warily as if he'd sighted a war party. Yet none of them could do a thing but walk on to a meeting.

It was Lorna who broke the deadlock, stopping and pulling Dill to a stop. Her smile, though, was directed at Melissa, and she said sweetly, 'Well, hello there. Isn't it a lovely evening for walking?'

Twig wanted to say that it had been until that moment, but Melissa smiled as sweetly as Lorna did and murmured, 'Isn't it? You're looking marvellous, Lorna. And Dill – how are you?'

Dill hadn't bothered to hide his surly displeasure. But, questioned, he managed to grunt, 'Good enough.'

'And how's Stringer?' Twig heard himself asking. 'He ever heal?'

If Dill had been before a jury, the look on his face would have convicted him. It was so pronounced that Lorna looked at him in curious surprise. Cornered, Dill had to say something, and he grunted again.

'Stringer who? Hames? Healed from what?'

'Heard he bit off more than he could chew a while back and got bunged up.'

'Ain't seen him in a coon's age. So I couldn't tell you.' Dill looked awkwardly at Lorna. 'I reckon we better get on. I want to talk to Oak before he hits the hay.'

They went on up the path. Lorna still looked puzzled, and Twig wished she knew what had been behind that exchange.

He went on with Melissa, and a few steps

later she said, 'If you think I knew we'd meet them, you're crazy. But it didn't do you any harm as far as she's concerned. Maybe it'll persuade her she had better fix her fence. It was foolish, though, to jab Dill about Hames.'

'I couldn't stand for his evening to be pure pleasure. And he sure proved he sent Stringer to get me or knows who did.'

'We already knew that, and he's not going to let Lorna learn of it from him. Twig, you've got to get over your habit of going off half-cocked.'

He glanced at her. She was right, and the problem of Stringer Hames was nothing like the problem he might have to face in the scablands. He decided to tell her about the curious packtrain of rock salt he had trailed in there, and he did.

'That sure is odd,' Melissa agreed. 'And I think you're mostly right about it.'

'Why mostly?'

'I doubt that Dill's running it, anymore. It's my guess that it's taken to running him.'

'How come?'

'Why should he steal what he thinks he can marry and get out of having to divide?'

That Dill might have lost control of things was a new thought to Twig. Yet it made sense. His mind ran over the men on the east-side spreads who might have taken charge. The foremen at Injun and Rock creeks would be good followers in a crooked game but they weren't leaders of that kind. Sid Lublin at Crab Creek was another breed of cat, a type Oak wouldn't have tolerated if he could have got out enough to acquaint himself with the men working on the ranges there.

'Then maybe it wasn't Dill who tried to get me killed,' he mused. 'Even if he does know about it.'

'I hope it wasn't,' Melissa said. 'I'd hate to think your father could be fooled that bad by a man.'

Twig realized that he hoped the same thing.

While they walked and talked, all but the last light had faded out of the sky. They turned back and were silent all the way to town. They reached the wharf boat and packet to find that Abner and the boat crew were still away. Twig hoped Melissa would ask him to sit with her on her own deck again. But when they reached it, she went on to the door where she told him good night and went in, shutting the door between them.

His cabin up on the texas had cooled off enough to be comfortable. Lacking anything better to do, Twig went to bed only to lie awake wondering how late Dill would be allowed to stay at the Tully house. And how Oak felt about what was undoubtedly a growing romance between Dill and Lorna. When finally he fell asleep it was to dream of the way Lorna's eyes had accused him the night he told Oak he planned to become a riverman.

Dill was winning out through a fidelity that embraced the rankest kind of treachery.

Twig didn't understand what Melissa had meant about Lorna's fixing her fence until midmorning Sunday. Abner and his men had put in a hard night and were still sleeping in their own quarters. Apparently Melissa was catching up on sleep, too. The note arrived in the grubby hands of a town urchin. Twig gave him a dime, ignored his impish grin, and waited until the boy had gone ashore to open the envelope. The boy had already got over that the message came from a girl. And the girl was the one Twig hoped it would be.

'I know why you haven't felt like coming to the house,' he read eagerly. 'But Oak went up to the Peshastin with Dill this morning. So?'

It had been good indeed for her to see him walking with another girl, and Twig's spirits, which had been below sea level, were soon in the clouds. He pulled up a bucket of water from the river, shaved, and took a water-slopping bath. But he was still wearing the boat cap and landlubber shoes, a little stubbornly, when he hurried up the main street and over to the Tully house.

He found Lorna on the vine-covered front porch, and she gave him a smile that was prepared to grow warmer or vanish, whichever was expedient. It was natural for her to feel restraint, but he found himself growing wary.

'Well, you did come,' she said. 'I wasn't sure you would.'

'Why not?'

He could have sat down in the porch swing with her but he took the banister so he could look at her. Her thick dark hair was in a bun at the back of her neck, and she had put on a pale blue dress he had never seen.

'Well,' she said hesitantly, 'I already wondered how much Melissa had to do with your foolishness. And after seeing you with her last night–' Lorna lifted her shoulders in a shrug.

'Why–' All at once it seemed insulting to Melissa for him to brush her aside as of no importance. 'I don't know what you mean by my foolishness. Or why you'd think she had anything to do with what I've done.'

'She's a very pretty girl. And you're being very foolish. I don't mean to lecture you, but I do want to talk things over while Oak isn't here.'

'He wouldn't thank you for it.'

'He sure wouldn't,' Lorna agreed. 'But why don't you cut it out and come back where you belong? Oak misses you and so do I.'

'You didn't look very lonesome last night.'

'Because I went for a walk with Dill? It happens he's the only one around I can get out of the house with, anymore.'

'You never showed any preference for me while I was around that I recall.'

'I know.' Lorna dropped her glance to the hands in her lap. 'I – well, I wouldn't say this if things hadn't come to such a pass. But I'm sorry I played you against each other. It's just something a girl does.'

'You mean I'd have the inside track, Lorna? If I come back?'

'Yes.' She nodded her head. 'You would.'

'Let's nail it down, Lorna,' Twig said harshly. 'If I dropped everything and patched things up with Oak, would you marry me? Yes or no?'

She didn't want it to be that definite. He could see her struggling within herself. But after a moment she nodded and said, still without looking at him, 'Yes. I would.'

'Because you think so much of Oak? Or because you think enough of me?'

'Both, I guess.'

He said with a hurting throat. 'Well, I can't do it even for that, but don't think it's easy to turn down.'

Her voice was small. 'You'll never come back?'

'Maybe not. But if I do, it'll be because I

choose to and not because I was enticed.'

Lorna pulled back her head, but instead of showing anger her eyes glinted with tears. 'You might as well leave,' she said. 'We're not getting anywhere.'

He got to his feet and started for the steps, then stopped to look at her again. 'The offer withdrawn?'

'No. It stands. If you don't take too long about it.'

He walked down the long street with hot, unseeing eyes. He had to forget she had held out herself as a reward for his coming back to OT under the old terms. If he thought about it too long, he might do it. She was in his blood just that bad. No matter if what she really loved was neither him nor Oak but OT. A cattle kingdom with Oak the king and himself the princely heir apparent. His desire for her was just that blindly crazy.

CHAPTER THIRTEEN

Twig came to the river across from Brown's Landing in the last of a starlit May night and dismounted for the long swim he had to make. On the far side the *Chief* rode on its lines in the now high water. He had left it on its previous trip up and since then had spent the daylight of two days skulking on the Injun Creek range.

Roundup was getting under way there. Since there were no calves to brand on the feeder ranch, the work consisted of grading and regrouping the steer herds, throwing back strays, and getting the spring tally. This made it a fluid operation that gave the cattle thieves every chance to do their work. Yet the yield of all his efforts and the chances he had taken had been nothing whatsoever. The work there went on according to its regular pattern. He had ridden the northern edge of the scablands several times and found no sign of steers having been run in.

Twig thought of this while he hung his gun rig high on the saddle horn to keep it dry. Then he followed the horse he had borrowed from Judah through the shallows to swimming depth. The water was bitterly cold even at that season for it was snow melt from the mountains. It made him think of the frigid morning when he had helped Dill cross part of the new feeders. But this time there were no cattle to hamper him, and he made it over quickly to come out dripping and with chattering teeth.

The landing was still abed, and nothing showed on the *Chief* but its mooring lights. Thoroughly at home there now Twig took the horse to the barn, rubbed it down with gunnysacks, and gave it a feed of oats. But he was still miserably cold himself when finally he went aboard the steamboat, slipped off his wet clothes, and toweled himself warm.

By then day was breaking, and he could hear others stirring on the boat. But they wouldn't be so busy getting ready to shove off that morning. Twice a week since the first of May one or the other of the Brown boats rode the high water of the Okanogan as far north as Pogue's Landing. So there was much less freight, express, and mail to be handled at Brown's Landing and fewer passengers to spend the night at the hotel.

When he had dressed in dry clothes, Twig went ashore to see Judah. The portly head of the Brown family was having breakfast in the hotel dining room, and Twig accepted an invitation to join him. While they ate he made his two-word report to Judah, 'No luck.'

'Just the same,' Judah said stubbornly, 'there's somethin' too peculiar about that salt to dismiss. Don't give up on it yet.'

'I don't aim to,' Twig said, although he was more discouraged than he sounded. 'At least till I've gone into the scabs myself and looked around.'

'You know what it's like in there?'

'No,' Twig admitted. 'I didn't know why at the time but Dill never would let me go over on the east side much.'

'From what the Indians tell me, them scabs are mean,' Judah warned. 'Even without a small army of men who'd like to kill you.' He pushed away his plate and stuck a cigar in his mouth, then said around the cigar, 'Abner tells me you've took to the water like a duck. The way business grows I been thinkin' I might even build another boat. It could take the Okanogan run when the water's up and work extra on the Columbia the rest of the year. I'd need a man to run it.'

Twig put down his fork and lifted his mug of coffee. He knew he was being nudged, though gently, to make up his mind whether he would stick to the river or go back to OT. Judah had been willing to gamble, but it wasn't fair to keep him dangling too long for Judah's own affairs moved on.

Stalling, Twig said, 'If you mean me, I'm not ready for that by quite a while. I stand wheel watches now, and I've learned a thing or two about the boat and the river. But that's a long ways from being ready to take command.'

'I know that. But it would take a while to knock another boat together and get the machinery shipped in and everything set.'

Twig sighed, genuinely torn between the two prospects. 'Abner's convinced me the cattle business is due to shrink,' he commented, 'even if it manages to stay alive. How long do you think the river trade'll last?'

'The rest of your workin' life,' Judah said with conviction. 'They're talkin' about a new railroad to run right through the Wenatchee country to the Sound. They're bound to build it in a few more years. But it'll help instead of hurt us, because you'll be an old man before they'll build spurs into the country our boats trade in.'

The day when he would be an old man seemed as distant as Kingdom Come to Twig. But his day of decision had become immediate and was pressing hard. 'I'll let you know pretty soon, Judah,' he promised.

'Sure. Take your time.'

The *Chief* was ready to cast off by the time Twig was back aboard. He helped pull in the gangplank, then Abner blew the whistle, kicked the gong, and they were sliding out into the swollen current and making around the bend.

The run to Wenatchee City in high water made Twig think of being in a toboggan chute with greased runners and no brake. While many of the rock and snag hazards had been drowned out, lethal races had taken their place, many of which had to be lined both ways. Again there were whirlpools that threatened to pitch the steamer out onto the rocky shore. The landings were difficult and dangerous for, as Abner said, the problem wasn't how to get to one but how to get stopped there without overshooting by a couple of miles.

The run that day was no better and no worse than they all had been of late. But with the days grown long, the *Chief* was tied up in Wenatchee City well before evening. Twig helped with the unloading, for he hadn't been given an officer's status and exemptions as yet. The upbound freight gathered that day was trundled aboard. The boat crew ate the day's meal, then they were all at leisure for the night.

Twig didn't know what to do with his own spare time. After that one Saturday evening of being friendly, Melissa had become distant and aloof again. He yearned to see Lorna once more in spite of the danger of his surrendering to her terms and offer. But if Oak had been away from the house again, she hadn't bothered to send word.

So again he found himself all alone on the

packet, and it was there that Melissa found him not long after Abner had left. Twig hadn't even expected to be invited down to the shade of her deck, much less to have her appear in the doorway of his cabin. But that's what she did, although he saw at once that she wasn't looking for company. Her face was even more somber than it had been the past couple of weeks.

Melissa said without preamble, 'Your girl came to see me this afternoon.'

'Now, which of my girls was that?'

'You know who I mean, and she left word for you. Your father wants you to come over to see him. Tonight. She said to tell you it's very important.'

'Oak?' Twig said. That made it something else. 'He sick?'

'She didn't say, but I doubt it.'

It was clear that Melissa didn't think much of the idea. He wondered how she could know that there was a campaign on to get him to throw in his hand and return to OT. But Oak's sending for him could be anything but that.

'Well, thanks,' he said.

'You going?' she asked.

'I've got to see what it's about.'

'I guess.'

Melissa turned and went away. Twig waited until she was back in her quarters before he left the steamer himself. The sun had dropped behind the bare, brown hills, and a blued softness had come to the valley and river and town. In midweek it was a lazy, nearly deserted street, and he walked quickly to the corner where he turned. Even as he came in sight of the Tully house he saw that the front porch was empty. He started worrying, for Oak in warm weather nearly always sat out there.

Twig climbed the steps and for yet another time suppressed the urge to knock on the door. His father was in the sitting room and by himself. He looked the same as he always had except sterner. Neither of them offered a greeting and for a moment they just regarded each other.

'Well, Oak,' Twig said finally. 'I heard you sent for me.

Oak nodded. 'And I never thought I would.' He had to stop and clear a frog from his throat. 'But Lorna kept at me till I gave in. Set down.'

Twig sensed that there would be more peace overtures and that again he wouldn't like the terms. Oak was bending his neck this way only for Lorna's sake, and even then it was painful to him. Oak waited for some kind of comment and when he didn't get it went on.

'Busy season's come again. Dill ain't complained, but pretty soon he's gonna have two full-sized jobs on his shoulders. We're gonna need you on the trail again.'

'You talked this over with Dill?' Twig asked.

Oak scowled. 'I don't talk over my family affairs with him.'

'Oak,' Twig returned, 'you've talked me over with him since I was knee-high to a blow fly. All you know about me you got from him.'

'So you still got that in your craw.'

'I'm not the one who put it there, and I'm not the one who can pull it out.'

'All right.' Oak scrubbed his hand over his face. 'I don't see your point, but I'll allow it. You handle the trail work again this season, and I'll see Dill keeps his nose out of it.'

'That's not good enough.'

'There's more. Lorna tells me the only thing standin' between you two is this thing that's got hold of you and raised hell.'

'I guess so,' Twig admitted. 'She let on that way the other day, at least.'

'She meant it. She told me about that and that you took it wrong. She cares for you. But she cares for me, too, and she don't want to have to choose between us.'

'I don't call that enough, Oak. She can't marry us both.'

'Then maybe you'd like a choice.' Oak's jaw set, and he was silent through several breaths. 'I always hoped to see somethin' come between you two. The day it does –

well, that's the day I'll hand OT over to you and turn myself out to pasture. What more could I do to pull the things outta your craw you say you can't get out yourself?'

Twig was so unprepared for an offer that sweeping he blinked his eyes. But there was plenty wrong with it. Not only had Oak been talked into making it. He was only upping the bribe Lorna had offered, and nowhere was there a simple, honest recognition of the man who was Oak's son.

'Well?' Oak said.

'That's the carrot,' Twig said, shaking his head. 'The biggest cattle outfit and the most beautiful woman in the Territory. I think I know what Lorna wants, but that's between her and me. You only want to keep a Tully at the head of OT and arrange so there can be another generation. You might as well unlimber your stick, because I won't come back on terms like that.'

'Then what in God's name will fetch you?'

'Your respect. And, if there's any of it hidden in all this, Lorna's real love. I don't aim to be nothing but your link with the future and hers with OT. So what's the stick?'

'All right.' Oak's voice rose like a peal of thunder. 'You want the stick, you'll get it. I'll give you a week. You be back then ready for work or, by God, you're through for good. I mean it. I never meant anything more.'

Twig got to his feet. 'That go for Lorna?'

'Yes,' a voice said behind him. 'It goes for Lorna.'

He swung around. Lorna had appeared from somewhere and stood in the archway from the hall. The eyes that had been so pleading not long before were now as glacial as Oak's. He knew she had eavesdropped all the while and had heard what he had said in reference to her, too. He knew she accepted that as final that the little there had been between them was all over now.

He walked past her to the front door of the house, then stopped to look at her again and tip his head toward his father.

'Why don't you marry him?' he asked. 'Give him a new heir and get what you want, to boot.'

She gasped, and Twig went out.

He walked through streets grown dark and had reached the foot of the gangplank that would carry him from the wharf boat to the *Chief* when something caused him to turn his head. Melissa was sitting in one of the barrel chairs on her own deck. She was looking toward him but hadn't spoken. He turned and went over to where she was and sat down in the other chair.

'You were always right,' he said. 'She'll marry whatever man can set her up as the mistress of OT.'

'I thought the showdown was coming,' Melissa said quietly. 'And I was scared to

183

death you'd flunk the test.'

She asked no questions, but Twig found himself telling her about Lorna's sending for him that Sunday and promising to marry him if he would walk back into the harness from which he had escaped. And what Oak had offered to do if there was such a marriage.

'I feel kind of sorry for her, though,' Melissa said.

'She wanted it to be you. That's why she tried so hard to make it you. For what comfort it is to you, I think she cares.'

'But not enough.'

'No, not enough. But it won't be Oak. Even if she was willing, it would be so outlandish Oak couldn't help seeing right about her. As far as you went.'

'I thought I went pretty far.'

'I'd say she played a cold-blooded pat hand tonight,' Melissa pointed out. 'She couldn't lose. If they lured you back, she won. If you refused, she knew Oak'd fly off the handle and disown you completely. The way she sees it, she's still won for she's the only one left for Oak to leave everything to.'

'Then she doesn't have to marry Dill.'

'She does. She and Oak both know she can't run OT. It takes an experienced and competent man to do that, and who'll be left around but Dill?'

'He's welcome,' Twig said.

'I don't think you're that lighthearted about it.'

'No, I'm not,' Twig admitted. 'Dill's rotten. I've got to prove that for Oak's sake, even for hers. Tell me something, Melissa. Do you want me to stay with the river?'

'I only want you to do what you want to do, Twig.'

'Could you give up the river and live on a cattle spread?'

'Why?'

'Wondered.'

'Yes,' Melissa said. 'I could with someone who's really a man.'

CHAPTER FOURTEEN

Dill pulled down his horse and quickly lifted the field glasses from the case on his saddle. Off to his left and announced mainly by dust the Rock Creek men were working a herd of cows and calves picked up in the morning gather. But what had caught his eye was a lone mounted figure that had been moving toward him and then had cut off at a slant to the right. Maybe the change of direction hadn't been to avoid him, but Dill always checked on such things. The minute he had thumbed the glasses into focus, he didn't know if he was glad or sorry that he had.

The stringbean rider in the droopy, peaked hat was Stringer Hames. It wasn't unusual for him to put in an appearance on the east-side ranches, but his doing so just then and the furtiveness of his manner instantly filled Dill with worry. They were about to take the first cut of cattle and he had found no way to prevent them. He put away the glasses and rode on toward the cutting ground at a trot. Presently he looked back to see that Hames had turned off into some scabby ground and disappeared.

When one of the first men he saw at the branding fire was Sid Lublin, Dill knew he had correctly interpreted Hames's presence. There was no good reason for Lublin to be here at the brood roundup when he was running his own on Crab Creek. He stood with Trink Neysmith and both of them watched with guarded eyes while Dill rode up to them and dismounted.

'I seen Hames cutting off across the flat from here,' Dill announced. 'Went out of his way to miss me. What business did he have here?'

Neysmith shifted his feet uneasily, but Lublin grinned.

'Thought I told you about that,' Lublin said easily. 'Stringer and me're goin' partners in the Idaho panhandle.'

'That's a long ways from here.'

'So it is.'

'Then answer my question. What's he doin' here?'

'Well, he's here to get some cattle. And now that you're here, too, you can give him a bill of sale so he won't have any trouble on the trail. His boy's are vent-branding in the big coulee right now. But they'll be through in a few days and ready to trail.'

Dill didn't answer, for he knew he would have to do whatever Lublin demanded. At least it would be a relief to get the stuff that had been snowballing in the scabs for weeks out of there. Lublin had tapped the Rock Creek herds of every critter that could be written off without arousing Oak's suspicions and thrown in more. But once they were gone, the bleeding and worry would be over until another spring. By then – well, once he had Lorna he would hold an ace of his own.

He knew that his efforts to boss the east-side work had become so much a matter of playing an empty part that he gave the men there plenty to laugh about in private. Yet his pride forced him to carry it out. He watched the branding a while and chewed out a roper for throwing a calf too hard. He looked at the tally book as if he thought it was honest and rode out to the herd and looked it over. Empty, every bit of it, for these men were running things their way and knew it. They had in effect stolen the whole damned east side.

He didn't want to stay with them overnight. But to keep them from thinking they had him buffaloed completely he lingered to eat supper at the chuckwagon. Then, after signing his name to a bill of sale Lublin held out and which he dared not read, Dill rode out toward Badger Mountain. His stomach was queasy with fear, for the minute he signed his name he had transferred the main danger from their shoulders to his.

He slept that night on the open range and

the next morning rode on to Wenatchee City. He stopped to see Oak, as he always did when he passed through, to learn that Oak had driven up to the Peshastin the afternoon before.

'He's terribly upset,' Lorna said. 'He had to be doing something, I guess.'

Dill's throat was dry as dead tumbleweed. 'What upset him?'

'Twig,' Lorna said bitterly. 'Who else?' Then she smiled like she wanted to forget it and added, 'I'm glad to see you. I've been so depressed. You haven't had your breakfast, have you?'

'No, but I can catch a bite at the restaurant.'

'You'll do no such thing.'

Dill followed her into the kitchen, eaten by curiosity but afraid to pry too openly. He had a feeling that it would spill out of her, so he drank coffee patiently while she made breakfast for just the two of them. He thought his arrival had cheered her, and that was a good sign.

But his patience had worn thin before she decided to talk about it. She hadn't eaten more than a few bites of biscuit smeared with jam. When she spoke finally, it was with an intensity that made him forget the biscuits, bacon, and gravy on his own plate.

'It goes to show what a fool a girl can make of a man.'

'Well,' Dill said. 'What fool and what girl?'

'Twig and that Brown chit. She's turned his head completely.'

Dill frowned. The jealousy she no longer tried to hide hardly flattered him. He said, 'You'll have to cut the deck deeper than that.'

'I know. Twig came to see Oak the other night and offered to come back providing Oak turned OT over to him lock, stock, and barrel. I guess he thought he had cut Oak up so bad he could write his own ticket. I bet she put him up to it. Maybe it was what she had in mind when she enticed him away.'

'What did Oak say to that?' Dill asked in a hollow voice.

'Can't you guess? Oak told him to get out of the house and never come back again.'

'And what did you tell him?'

'I said that went for me, too.'

Dill laid down his fork and leaned back in his chair in relief. Twig was out of it finally as completely as if Stringer's slug had eliminated him, and this way was safer if not better. That didn't mean, Dill knew, that he himself was in completely. But if he played his cards right he would be, all the way.

'Well, I'm sorry to hear it,' he said. Then he added quickly, 'I mean about him and Oak. Even if the kid was a disappointment to Oak, I know he cared for him. But all I can say is hallelujah when it comes to you giving Twig his time. I was sure scared you'd marry him.'

'There wasn't a chance,' Lorna scoffed. 'At least, after I realized he'll never grow up. It was Oak's feelings I worried so about. But now Oak seems to have his eyes open, too.'

'I wonder,' Dill said, pressing at last, 'what that's gonna do to me and you.'

'Oak's not saying.' She knew what he meant, met his eyes, and smiled. 'But you can count on it. He'll be loyal to those that have been loyal to him. And he won't back down on his stand against Twig. So your job's safe.'

'But Oak can't run OT much longer. He's too far along in years.'

'So what happens afterward?' Lorna had changed miraculously from depression to good spirits. 'He wants me in his family all the more now. Lately he's talked to me about the past. He was deeply in love with my mother, you see, and pretty cut up when she married my dad. It's like he's got her finally in me, although he doesn't love me the same way. Besides, he feels indebted.'

Dill forgot his half-eaten breakfast, intensely interested in this hidden corner of Oak's life. 'He come from Nevada,' he prompted. 'I guess this happened down there.'

Lorna nodded. 'The Comstock. It was

new and raw and wild, then, with a hundred going broke for every one that hit it. My father hit it.'

'Oh?'

'And lost it all inside of two years. Then he died, and my mother went back to what she'd been doing to make a living. That was working in a saloon. It wasn't easy on her, or me either while I grew up. For she got too old for that and, well, there was only one way left to make a living.'

'Then how come you came here to live?'

'When my mother learned she was about to die, she wrote Oak a letter. I was grown, but I wasn't trained to earn a living except the way she had. She was afraid I'd wind up in her footsteps, and I probably would have.'

Lorna looked at Dill with a bitter smile. 'What do you think of me now?'

'You didn't have a thing to do with it,' Dill said. 'Anyhow, what difference could it make to me?' For the first time Dill felt comfortable with her. He said, 'I'll show you how I feel by askin' you again. Will you marry me?'

'Yes.' She nodded her head. 'I will.'

It was done that coolly, with them sitting across the table from each other and not so much as touching hands. Dill understood that she was no more after marriage for its own sake than he was, that they simply had reason to pull together and that thereafter they would.

'Will you do it right away?' he asked. If she would he was out of the woods.

She considered that a moment, then nodded again. 'Whenever you want.'

'Good. Do whatever women do to get ready. I'm in an itch to have you.'

For a moment he had an awful fear that she had feeling for Twig no matter what she had said about him. Her eyes regarded him for an instant with something in them that pushed him away. Then she shrugged her shoulders and smiled.

When he rode out of town and headed for the Peshastin, Dill felt like a new man. It would take the marriage to cinch his place with Oak, but Lorna's promise would be a help in itself. So when he reached the westside ranch he went at once to the house. Oak was there, sitting on the front porch in his wheelchair and looking shockingly old and frail. It struck Dill that the man had come here because it was more like home to him than the town house. The place where he had lived with his wife and became a father and laid the foundation of a cattle empire. Like he'd come back in hopes it would help him figure out where things had gone wrong.

When they had exchanged greetings, and he had reported the work going well, Dill decided to get to the heart of it without wasted breath. He said bluntly, 'Oak, I hope this meets with your approval. I'm gonna marry Lorna. She promised me at the house this morning. It's gonna be right away.'

For a moment he thought Oak hadn't heard him, for Oak kept staring off into the distance. Way off there a dust showed that a roundup crew was moving steers, and this was about as close as Oak could get to such work anymore. Then Oak turned his head to look at Dill with eyes that showed no pleasure.

'Right away? Why?'

'Well, Oak,' Dill said with an uneasy laugh, 'when a man's won a purty girl, he wants her. Is it gonna be all right with you?'

'She's of age,' Oak said, and he shrugged.

'I guess you're kind of cut up,' Dill said uncertainly. 'Lorna told me the latest on Twig.'

Oak cut him off. 'There's no need to discuss him.'

Dill saw in a moment of truth that a hollow had been left in Oak that he himself would never fill. It was rejection again, as crushing as the time Oak told him to take Twig and train him to fill his father's boots.

'No,' he said painfully. 'Except I want to say I'm sorry he turned out the way he did.'

Oak looked at him then, full and hard and for a long moment. 'Maybe,' he said harshly, 'he turned out a hell of a lot heftier than I ever knew. Or was allowed to know. That boy's got spine. It took plenty to turn down my offer and Lorna's offer and stick to what he believed in. Maybe it was nothing but spine that made him contrary so often.'

Dill had a feeling that an earthquake had shaken the valley. 'Your offer–?' he began.

'That ain't ranch business,' Oak snapped. 'And if Lorna's gonna marry you, her part in it don't matter.'

Dill realized Lorna had lied to him. He didn't know why. Lamely, he said, 'Well, I hope it don't make any difference in where I stand.'

'I need a man to run OT. You know how to run it. So don't worry about that.'

Oak looked away with an expression of dismissal so pronounced Dill turned numbly and walked out into the yard to his waiting horse. He had been stupid. In his drive to protect himself he had made things move much too fast for Oak. It would have been better if he'd let Lorna tell him about the marriage in her own good time. A marriage, Dill realized, that was part of the disappointment Oak felt.

CHAPTER FIFTEEN

Dawn sunlight lay on the rolling horizon beyond Link Sands's window, accenting the green of the new wheat. The lamp by which the settler had cooked breakfast was no longer needed, so Sands bent over to blow it out. When he looked at Twig again, he shook his lion's mane of hair.

'You're takin' too big a chance goin' into those scabs by yourself,' he said. 'It worried me all night. I better saddle me a horse and go along.'

'Thanks.' Twig grinned at him with more confidence than he felt. 'But you've stuck your neck out too far lending me a horse again if somebody happens to recognize it.'

'You let me worry about that. But I'm startin' to wish I hadn't sent you that tip.'

Twig clapped him on the arm and moved to the door. He was dressed in range clothes and wore the gun rig that had begun to feel natural to him. He said, 'I'll see you some-time after dark tonight. But if I don't make it for another night, don't worry. That's big country up there.'

'Luck,' Sands said, surrendering, and he offered his hand.

The settler had saddled the gelding that Twig had ridden before. It carried him swiftly against the sun until the cultivated patch of green earth was behind and desert range surrounded him again. He rode loosely in the saddle, although he meant to do the brashest thing he had tried yet.

Two days earlier the *Chief* had found the flag up at Pine Canyon and a note from Sands. All the note said was that the settler had something to tell him the first chance he got to come ashore. So Twig had left the boat on the down trip the next day. What Sands had had to report could mean much or nothing at all. The suspect country was much too far away for him to keep an eye on things there for himself. But he had seen something much closer to home that might be connected with it.

Part of the Rock Creek's roundup crew had been working along the base of Badger Mountain, and Sands had been over that way one day hunting sage hens. He had noticed something and taken a quiet look at it from cover. Instead of turning loose the stuff, when they were through with it, the punchers were holding it until they had cut out a lot of two- and three-year cows, either with calves on the ground or in the oven. That being a curious procedure, Sands had watched from his vantage point until they had driven this cut of about thirty head off to the northeast. Only then had they turned the rest of the gather loose.

Hearing that, the night before, Twig had blinked his eyes. 'It sure *is* unusual. But how could they make money out of stuff like that?'

'Well, they wouldn't tempt a fancy price out of a butcher with it,' Sands said. 'But any rancher would like to own fine brood stock from OT. Everybody knows it's got the best built-up herds around.'

'Any rancher that would buy it from rustlers,' Twig retorted, 'would be crazy in the head. Beef steers disappear, but a cow's of no value unless she's kept alive and breeding.'

'True,' Sands admitted. 'But it kept nagging at me till I thought I'd better pass it on.'

'I'm glad you did,' Twig assured him. 'And it's worth lookin' into. If they're picking up that kind of critters on the Rock Creek side, it's no wonder I never scared up anything on the Injun Creek edge of the scabs.'

His intention, now, was to lose himself in the rough lands long before he reached the vicinity where he had seen the Rock Creek men take the stock salt. That would lessen the danger of running into somebody or of being seen without knowing it and riding into a trap. Yet it called for a lot of picky riding. The terrain itself wasn't so dangerous, but it was blind country, cut up by rims and buttes, coulees and washes. If he could cut it he would work eastward, and if there was brood stock hidden where they had taken the salt, he would have what he needed.

Midmorning found him in the first moraines, which he entered to follow in a slow swing southward and then back to the east. By noon he had come to the first of the grassy, interior meadows. It was empty, but maybe only from lack of water. He knew that such meadows chained from there for a great distance, and any of them could confront him with both evidence and sudden trouble. That meant taking a good look at each before he entered, and that slowed him down.

He picked on doggedly while the heat mounted until in early afternoon it came off the rocks like heat from a stove. He found shade in which to rest the horse while he ate a couple of cold biscuits and drank sparingly from the saddle canteen. He still had seen nothing, not even the tracks of stray animals or of a rider passing through. But his patient work had produced one result. If there was anything to be found in the scabs, it was confined to the east end where the Rock Creek punchers had taken the salt, and that helped tie things together.

He had underestimated the furnace heat that the day had begun to produce. The horse was showing the effects and the water in the canteen would hardly wet its throat. Twig had a strong feeling that he would need its best before he was out of this. So when he came to a dry cross coulee he rode north and emerged cautiously into the Injun Creek range. The roundup crews were done in that immediate vicinity, and he saw no sign of them. When presently he came to a wooded brook, he stopped to water the horse and loosen its cinch and let it graze awhile on the cured grass.

He had smoked a cigarette and was preparing to ride on when he saw the dust. Outside the dead air of the depressions there was a gentle breeze, enough to raise a go-devil in some dusty place. But he watched and, when the dirty spot grew larger, took the field glasses he had brought along out of their case. He had to wait minutes more before he was sure of a horse and rider ahead of the dust and heading straight for the scabs.

This was the first man since the packers he had seen have anything to do with the roughs, and excitement honed his alertness to a keen edge. He kept his glasses riveted on the figure, which grew larger and larger and all at once dinged a memory of moments even more intense. The rider was uncommonly thin and tall. Gone was the dirty sheepskin coat, but the battered hat was still there.

Twig knew that his big chance had finally come. Of all the people he knew, the one with the least honest business in that vicinity was Stringer Hames. He waited in tight-chested watchfulness while Hames came abreast and then vanished into the outlying formations of the roughs. Then he put away the field glasses, mounted and rode slowly until he cut the man's sign. Hames had been swallowed by the gap between two low, rocky buttes. Twig began to follow the tracks of the other horse, not hurrying. While they remained fresh, he needed no other guidance.

He found that the gap made a gradual descent on the other side of the twin buttes. As near as he could tell he was by then due across from where he had seen the Rock Creek men go in. He rode down the brushy grade into a pinching ravine. There was no sign of Hames having stopped his horse. The ravine broke into a box canyon with a sandy bottom that hadn't lent itself so well to recording the steps of the other horse. Fortunately there was no fork or place where Hames could have left the canyon. The heat of the rocky walls had again grown intense and ennervating.

Then all at once he was in a deep canyon with close, nearly vertical walls. This warned him that a coulee would break ahead of him at any moment. But before this happened a spur came in from due east. Its bottom was littered with horse tracks but showed no sign of moving cattle. Yet he was getting closer to whatever he was to find, and he reined in for a moment to see what his ears could tell him. He heard nothing, so there were no cattle very near.

With little warning a twist in the canyon ended in open ground. Twig reined up quickly, still hidden but able to see into a small, grassed cirque. It told him nothing, and he would have to cross it to stay on Hames's heels. He wanted to take a good look before he tried that, so he dismounted, got the field glasses, and crept farther into the open.

The first thing he saw was smoke lifting against the opposite rim, and just this side of it there were several horses on picket. That was where Hames had gone, and Twig knew there were springs there and a camp. The cirque was too small to accommodate anything but those few horses, and what he saw had more the look of a hideout for men. He focused the glasses on the spot where the smoke originated.

The magnification let him see Hames again very plainly. The man had got himself coffee at the fire and was drinking it while, from the looks of it, he carried on a spirited conversation with the three other men in sight. There were more than that many horses on hand and, from the rather large equipage at the camp, some of them were pack animals. So, if these fellows were prepared to travel, it was ten to one they were to take charge of the cattle that had to be somewhere closeby.

Twig swung his glasses on around the walls of the cirque. The only break, besides the one where he stood, was off to the south. His brow knit thoughtfully, for he knew he had to go on yet couldn't possibly cross the cirque unseen. All he could do was backtrack and try to find a way around.

He knew from the reach of the shadows that the afternoon was slipping away. He went back to the gelding and a moment later was riding quietly back along the deep canyon. Now that he knew more about it, he realized there was a chance of somebody else coming in the way Hames had. So he watched the way ahead of him as painstakingly as he had when he came in. He met no one but didn't find a way out of the slot until he had almost resumed to the buttes between which he and Hames had entered the roughs. There he found himself able to climb to a bench west of the cirque. To that point his own horse tracks were confused by many others. Now he stitched a lone, new line sure to be followed if it was discovered. He knew he would need plenty of luck to investigate the situation as thoroughly as he must without stirring up a cyclone of trouble.

In another ten minutes he knew he would need luck just to make his way around Hames's hideout. Time and again the table that elevated him broke up in jagged, unpassable falls that forced him to hunt a way down and another way up on the far side. Once he came to a patch of shale so rotten he was afraid he would start a slide so noisy it would bring disaster down upon his head. But he lightfooted his way over, leading the nervous gelding, and afterward was rewarded by easy going for a while.

Climbing out of a gully that had given him new trouble, somewhat later, he found himself on another bench so flat and smooth it could have been used for a racetrack. The significant feature was the sharp line of its far edge across the southern sky. He knew something huge and deep lay over there and rode toward to the edge of the rim rock with a quickened heart.

And there it all was, a hidden meadow large enough to hold a small cattle ranch, and there were enough cows and calves scattered on its bottom to stock it. He stood marveling, for apparently the place was known only to men thoroughly familiar with the country from working the adjoining ranges. It probably had been used before for hiding beef steers lifted off the Injun Creek and Crab Creek grasslands until they could be safely disposed of.

At Sands's shack he had been unable to fathom how a rancher could be foolish enough to buy stolen brood stock. The field glasses explained it. The brands of the cows immediately off from him had been vented. That was what Hames and his men had been doing here and why the cattle had been held so long before being moved out of the country. Whoever bought the stuff, or was acquiring it at no cost, would have a bill of sale to authenticate the vents. Twig had to admire the cleverness of whoever had figured it out. It certainly had thrown him off the track, and without Sands's chance tip he still wouldn't have caught on.

Yet he knew that his discovery could be of great value or of none at all. The thieves wouldn't let go of this rich haul if they could help it. Yet to escape being caught redhanded they had only to scatter it back on the Rock Creek ranges, so thoroughly mixed with other stuff the vents would go unnoticed, until after the heat was off. Yet there were factors in his own favor. What he had seen with his own eyes, coupled with what Judah Brown saw when he caught Cultus Joe crossing the Indian reservation, was damning evidence. It ought to open Oak's eyes at least to the possibility that he had been brazenly cheated by a man he had trusted.

If he could so persuade Oak, all Oak needed to do to uncover what undoubtedly were large shortages was order another and surprise roundup run by a man he knew he could trust. That would show up the crooked books and false reports he had never had reason, himself, to question. Yet Twig's spurt of optimism was soon over. Oak had grown stubborn when it came to believing anything his son had to say against Dill Humminger. To make sure he got results, Twig decided to add a third voice to his and Judah's. He would work his way back to Sands's homestead, accept his offer of help, and bring him in here. Coupled with the OT brooders Sands had seen picked off the Rock Creek range, that would make testimony to overwhelm even a man with Oak's blind trust.

Having seen all he needed to see himself, Twig pulled back from the rim, made his way to cover, and then considered how to get out of the scabs. It would be safer not to try to leave the way he had come on. Yet that set up the problem of making his way through unknown badlands in the fading day and partly at night. And it would have to be accomplished on a horse already tired and which he had no intention of abusing.

While he smoked a cigarette, a third possibility came to mind. This coulee was where they had brought the stock salt to use to settle the cows as they were brought in. If he could make his way down and across, he would find a fairly easy place to leave the scabs where he had seen the packers enter. That would bring him out on the Rock Creek range. But he could wait until dark to go on, for he would have only a beeline to ride through known and open country to reach Sands's shack. This posed its own dangers, yet the advantages outweighed them.

He set about finding a way down to the bottom. This didn't disclose itself until he had reached the coulee's west end, and then it would have to be a descent over shale even more rotten than he had crossed previously. This would be dangerous, yet a study of the far rims through the field glasses showed him nothing better. He knew he had to take his chances and go down there at once.

The gelding thoroughly disliked the idea and began to balk even as it moved gingerly downward into the deep notch. When it got down to the loose rock it balked completely, and for the first time in his life Twig overrode a horse's judgment and forced it on with his spurs. He knew at once the enormity of his mistake for the loose, crumbled rock proved even more unstable than it had looked. Even as the gelding's hooves bit into it, hatfuls went tumbling downward, loosening more on the way.

Twig changed his mind instantly and attempted to turn the animal gently and ease it back to more solid footing. It was too late. There was more slippage when the gelding tried to come around, which frightened it into a springing leap. Its hind legs went out from under it, and Twig had a lightning memory of Oak going down such a slide to be crippled for life. In his own case the horse kept its balance a second or so longer, letting him hurl himself from the saddle on the upslope side. Then he and the horse were both tumbling downward in a growing avalanche of dust and rock.

Beyond bruises and abrasions all over him, he wasn't hurt, but the gelding didn't stop until it was well below him. Even as Twig picked himself up he saw the animal try to get to its feet and sink down again with a throaty complaint. The dawning truth was like a blow on the head, and for a moment Twig stood swaying with shut eyes. Then, dreading every step on the still treacherous detritus, he began to work down to the horse. He saw before he reached it that it was more than a case of the animal's being lamed. Bone stuck out through the bloody flesh between its near stifle and hock.

Remorse had to wait, for his situation was desperate. Not only had he put himself afoot with his hurried recklessness, but the horse couldn't be moved, then or later, nor could help be brought to it, very soon, under the circumstances. Twig's first thought was of this and the demand it imposed on him because he couldn't leave it there to suffer in pain and thirst and hunger in the heat. He knew he had to put it out of its misery before he tried to go on, and he knew the sound of a shot was more than apt to carry to the rustlers' camp in the cirque. Even if it did not, the body of the horse would soon be discovered to raise an alarm.

CHAPTER SIXTEEN

It was the hottest day of that spring, and Dill knew it would be no cooler in the rock scablands toward which he rode with Sid Lublin. At first he had intended to keep away from the east side until the latest raid on OT cattle was completely over. Yet the presence of the brooders in the scabs had haunted him, for the longer they remained the greater grew the danger of their being discovered. So he had returned to Crab Creek and argued Lublin into ordering them out immediately.

Lublin hadn't liked to be pushed but was shrewd enough to know he could push a man too far. This small triumph had stiffened Dill's spine. With Lorna promised to him he had everything he wanted and he was willing to go to any length to hold onto it. He had to put up with this one last raid. But that would have to be the end of it. Yet Lublin was still very much on hand, and so was his good friend Hames. So Dill contented himself, for the time being, with Lublin's agreement to start the brooders moving eastward at once, and he was along to see for himself that this happened.

Dill hadn't been in the scabs himself for

ages, so when they reached the edge he let Lublin take the lead. The heat mounted at once, coming off the rocks in a radiation that felt like a breeze. Dill pulled out his bandanna and mopped his face. 'The stuff sure must be losin' weight in there,' he muttered.

'Not like you'd think,' Lublin said. 'Where they are it's more open. Anyhow, that panhandle range will soon put 'em back in fine shape.'

'Free range and free cattle. You don't want much, do you?'

'Just all I can get,' Lublin said with a laugh. 'The same as you do.'

They had entered the roughs at an angle, but they were soon on what had become a much-traveled trail. Then all at once they were in a coulee whose wheeling size Dill had forgotten in the intervening years. He tried not to look at the cattle there, not because they made him feel guilty but because they scared him. Lublin led the way to the right, and presently Dill saw a cleft in the far rimrock.

Ten minutes later they were in the cirque and dismounting at the camp of Stringer Hames. The men there seemed surprised to see Dill but didn't comment. Hames was neither a friend nor an enemy of Dill so far. Dill didn't know the others.

'Well, boys,' Lublin said at once. 'You're

gonna move 'em out of here. Right now.'

'Pretty late in the day,' Hames said in surprise. 'What's the big hurry?'

'The man here,' Lublin said with a nod, 'has got boogered.'

'Any special reason, Humminger?' Hames asked.

Dill didn't get a chance to answer, for it was at that moment that the sound came, a distant but sharp puncturing of the silence around them. Every man present stared at somebody else. Finally one of the grimy-looking strangers said, 'That a shot?'

'Who'd shoot and what at?' Lublin scoffed and he moved a dismissing hand.

The others lacked his cocksureness, and Dill heeled around and stared against a blank rock wall to the west. Of them all, he seemed the only one with a sense of the direction from which the pinging percussion had come.

'What's over in that direction?' he said harshly, with a nod of the head.

'Nothin',' Hames answered, 'except a lot of mean country.'

'You better take a look.'

'Why not you?' Lublin cut in.

'This ain't my affair.'

'No? Buck, you're in this deeper than anybody here.'

'He's right,' Hames said. 'We better make sure.' He strode off toward his horse.

It wasn't fear of some kind of physical fracas that made Dill reluctant to accompany him. He was afraid of being seen here in circumstances so completely incriminating. Yet he was seeing for himself, from there on, and not trusting anybody else. He went over to his horse and swung up. Still looking dubious, Lublin followed suit. Since Hames and his bunch had to saddle up, Dill swung back toward the coulee with Lublin trailing him.

Out in the coulee Dill took a look to the west without seeing a thing that nature hadn't provided. He slowed while Lublin came up beside him, for Lublin had a gun and Dill hadn't worn one himself in years. Then they went on toward the western rimrock, which had a deep notch knocked out of its north end.

'Could anybody get down over there?' he asked Lublin.

Lublin shook his head. 'A squirrel'd be scared to try it.'

'Then maybe somebody fired a shot from the top,' Dill worried. 'Signalin' to somebody else.'

'And tip us off, too? Don't make jokes, Dill. It's too hot a day to laugh.'

But Lublin was less skeptical at the end of five minutes more. The patch of steel-gray colour three-quarters down the talus wasn't made by bleached rock, as it had first ap-

213

peared. Both men spurred their horses when they began to suspect this. By the time they dismounted at the foot they knew it was a saddled horse up there. The slide leveled to a less steep pitch toward the bottom and this had stopped the animal. Even so, they moved with extreme care while they worked their way up to where it lay.

The broken leg and bullet hole in the head told part of the story. 'You know that brand?' Dill said in a ragged voice.

'No.' Lublin was dead serious finally. 'But I think I know the critter. I've seen that settler over by Pine Canyon on one like it, anyhow.'

'Sands?'

'Yeah, that's it. And he's still around. He stood on this spot not over ten minutes ago, so he's got to be.'

The weeks of impotence, resentment, and fear goaded Dill now into a reckless temper. Hames and his men had come up by then. Round-eyed, they sat their horses at the foot of the slide. Dill raked them and then turned raging eyes on Lublin.

'You sons of bitches. Takin' your sweet time and just beggin' somebody to get onto you. So damned overconfident, you never even put a watch on the cattle. Now, by God, you're gonna scatter them critters back on the Rock Creek range. And, by God, you're gonna leave 'em and OT and me alone after this. Get at it, now. Get 'em outta here and back where they belong. You hear?'

He saw at once that he was on the edge of immediate trouble, without even a weapon of his own. Hames looked at him resentfully, and the men with him squared their shoulders.

'Not on your tintype.' Lublin's words punched out like shots. 'Just you simmer down, Buck, and do a little listenin' yourself. Sands ain't got any stake in this game. If he rode this dead cayuse, he was doin' it for somebody else. Who'd that be, you reckon?'

'You mean Twig Tully?'

'Who else, you chucklehead? We put too much work into this to throw it away, and it wouldn't do any good if we did. Once Oak's suspicions are aroused, the game is up for all of us, most of all you.'

'You're right,' Dill agreed, looking helplessly around. 'We've got to nail that settler.'

'It's my guess it's Twig, and Sands only loaned him this critter. And, by God, we've got to do what I've always wanted. Stop him before he gets to his dad, and stop him permanent. We can do it. He's on foot, and it's at least thirty miles to the river.'

Stringer Hames made a vigorous nod of the head. Killing Twig was something Dill had never been able to face, but now he saw the inevitability of it. A walking man couldn't make it to the river for many hours even if he was sound of limb. Dill couldn't see how anybody could have tumbled down that slide with the horse without being hurt. He remembered how badly Oak had been crippled. And if he got to the river, there were only a few places along those reaches where it could be crossed with the water as high as it was now.

Lublin had already seen this and taken charge. 'Stringer,' he yelled. 'You and your boys know these parts better than I do. Beat every bush and turn over every rock. Dill, you head for Injun Creek and get men to patrol the north side of the scabs and catch him if he tries to come out that way. I'll beat it to Rock Creek and pick up enough men for the south side. Watch the waterings. The son of bitch'll get thirsty. Hustle, now. We got to have everything covered by dark.'

Dill didn't like being bossed by a supposed underling even yet, but Lublin was thinking along the right lines. The first thing was to throw a ring around the scablands to keep their man from emerging while the scabs themselves were searched. Later, if the prey got away, men could be sent to the river to head him off at one of the few crossings. Heat, hunger, and exhaustion would be on their side, and they were safe until and unless word of this reached Oak.

He nodded his agreement to Lublin's instructions, adding, 'We better try first to

216

get a lead on which way he went. It's my guess he'd backtrack. If he didn't he'd stick to the rock so he wouldn't leave much sign.'

'Good idea,' Lublin agreed.

Nobody wanted to climb the treacherous slide, but somebody had to see whether the spy had doubled back or gambled on trying to get out by way of the coulee floor. Stringer Hames finally squared his shoulders and attempted it. Rock rolled with every uneasy step he took. Once he hesitated and looked back like he was about to crawfish. Then he went on and finally disappeared.

He showed up in only a moment to call, 'No boot tracks up here.'

Without a word Dill swung his horse and rode back toward the cirque, while Lublin hurried off in the other direction. By the time he reached Hames's camp, Dill was as coldly calculating as Lublin himself. He was going on the assumption that the spy had been Twig a more likely man for the role than the settler. And it would be like Twig to risk his own safety to put the badly hurt horse out of its suffering. A soft man, and yet one with a tenacity and courage Dill had never suspected. A sort of Oak Tully at that, although one of a gentler nature.

From the cirque Dill had only horse tracks to show him how to get out of the roughs on the north side. From there it was a two hour ride to Injun Creek headquarters even at the speed he traveled. It was evening by the time he got there. He told Cass Pickering what he wanted done, picked up a pistol and gun belt for himself, and headed back, drawn like a magnet to the danger that had been posed for him.

The light had grown gray and the shadows long by the time he reached the twin buttes. And on the far side of them he reined in to fix a more intent look on the horse tracks he had begun to watch as he rode. A single set of tracks stamped their way off from the trail to the right. They came from the direction of the cirque and could have been made by one of Hames's party, but they weren't quite fresh enough for that. He decided to follow them.

Before he had ridden very far he was sure that the dead gelding had made the prints. The design they slowly traced for him showed uncertainty and unfamiliarity with the area. The prowler had tried to get into the coulee, been forced back by the discovery of James's camp, and then had tried to work his way around. Dill followed stubbornly, although in the growing dusk it was hard to pick up the sign.

It was nearly dark by the time he came to the rim above the coulee where the intruder had come a cropper. He looked around carefully, for Hames had shown little taste for being up there and had spent as little time as possible. But Dill had had no better luck picking up a lead on the quarry when darkness forced him to give it up.

He knew that nightfall would bring in the Hames party, too, for they could accomplish nothing themselves after that. The thought of giving the quarry a whole night in which to slip away was unbearable but Dill knew he could do no more than they could. He had little taste for passing the night with them, but they might have made some progress by then, so he headed back toward their camp.

The Hames men were there, and so was Sid Lublin. They had picked up nothing, they said, and they looked less panicky about it than Dill had begun to feel.

'Ease up,' Lublin told him. 'The bastard ain't sprouted wings. He ain't even gonna get a horse under him without takin' it away from one of us. And he sure can't cross that many miles of flat, open country without bein' seen.'

Dill said nothing, hating them all with an intensity that was like acid eating his flesh. The only stake they had was easy pickings, which they would fight for to the last ditch. But if the thing went wrong all the way, they had only to head for yonder on fast horses and find a new game somewhere else. That let them feel this as an excitement and challenge, not as impending doom.

One of the men had been working at the cook fire. Presently he called, 'Come and get it,' and the others began to ladle out mulligan and pour themselves steaming cups of coffee. Dill was so thoroughly without hunger that the thought of eating repelled him. Yet he had had no food since morning, and knew the demands on him would be strenuous in the hours to come. So he made himself eat some of the stew and drink coffee. His confidence in the net that had been flung around the badlands was draining off by the minute.

The sounds of shots, that time, was too plain to be mistaken, and they came from the Rock Creek side. They all were those of one rifle, which meant that they came from a friendly gun. Every man at the camp sprang to his feet, and somebody yelled, 'The Rock Creek boys have flushed him! Come on!'

Dill was one of the first to reach his horse. Even while he tightened the saddle cinch a grin spread on his mouth. He heard Lublin saying he had left a man at that exit from the coulee. The fellow had got in enough shots to finish it, for there had been no contesting shots. Yet it didn't matter too much. If the quarry was that near, he was bound to be nailed before he could get away.

CHAPTER SEVENTEEN

Twig heard the rifle shots and flung a puzzled glance off to the south. He counted four of them in rapid succession, all seeming from the same gun. A fleeting, worried thought was that Link Sands had come blundering into trouble, still trying to help. That was out of the question, for he had told Sands clearly that he might not be back until the second night. There had been too many shots for it to be a call for help by one of his hunters. Then it came to him that one of them might have been spooked by something in the night and blazed away at it in a noisy, one-sided battle.

But Twig stayed where he was and waited to see, what happened next. This was a nest of rocks on the Injun Creek side of the coulee floor. It was a place Hames and his men had searched thoroughly, but he hadn't been there then nor for long now. Having betrayed his presence in the area by an act he couldn't bring himself to forego, he had known that wit alone could bring him through. So instead of making a desperate dash to get away, he had gambled on staying close to where he was until he knew if the

221

shot had been heard. And, if so, what Hames's hard-case outfit would do.

So he had worked his way back into the cleft at the top of the slide only to come partway down again. For from the higher elevation he had seen, off on the talus and hardly two hundred feet from the dead horse the short stub of a broken rock needle. The rotten rubble falling from above it had been parted by this to form a tiny hollow not discernible from below. After making sure he had left no telltale tracks, he had made his way into this, and barely in time. In another few minutes Dill and Lublin had come smoking in from the cirque, then shortly behind them Hames and his bunch.

Twig had kept his gun on them every minute, hardly daring to breathe. He had a particularly bad moment when Hames made his way to the top. But Hames hadn't looked toward him from up there and clearly wanted no more to do with the slide than he had to have. Twig had been near enough, afterward, to overhear Lublin's orders and be warned that the scabs were to be ringed by men, with Hames's men searching the interior.

From then until nightfall he had laid there in the rocks, drenched with sweat that stung his multiple abrasions and grown stiff and sore from his own bad fall. But once they searched the coulee floor, the Hames men pulled out of the immediate vicinity. And with it grown dark, Twig had come down onto the floor himself, carrying the saddle canteen and a couple of biscuits he had taken when he left the gelding. He had been about to strike off across the coulee to the Rock Creek exit when he heard the shots. Now that was cut off for him, at least for a while.

It was only moments later, when he heard hooves beating the earth and then saw the dark figures of riders from the cirque go streaking across to the Rock Creek outlet. He couldn't be sure how many there were, but it looked like the alarm had emptied the camp. And certainly it had created a diversion he might use to get out on the Injun Creek side. He hoped there would be one man left at the camp and one horse.

He walked with a limp because he had turned an ankle in the accident without noticing it until it had time to get sore. But he made himself walk swiftly, aiming toward the break leading to the rustlers' camp. When he reached the connecting passage it proved shorter than he had expected. At its far end he halted for a careful inspection. The fire lighted the camp, and he could see no one there and no horse. He knew why there now were no extra horses. They knew he was afoot and had made sure no un-watched horse was left where he could get hold of it. He sighed and went on.

Knowing he had a little time before Hames and his men returned he stopped at the camp, poured himself coffee, and drank it. It did a little to cut the drugging fatigue that weighted him. He drank a second cup, then looked at the tempting stew on the fire. Deciding he had crowded his luck enough, he went on. By then there was starshine to help him find his way, but it also made him more visible.

It seemed a long while after that when he saw ahead of him the twin buttes and stopped on their side to rest the ankle that had begun to throb. He had to have a horse before he went much farther. If there was a sentry watching this outlet, as there seemed to be on the Rock Creek side, there would also be a horse. He rubbed the painful joint gingerly, but that didn't help. Afraid that if he rested too long it would stiffen up and cripple him completely, he pushed to his feet.

He had to make a long detour around the left-hand butte, and this seemed to take him an hour. But when he began to curve back toward the avenue between it and its twin, he was on fairly open ground. He had his fist clenched on the grips of his gun by then, for he had no idea what to expect. He took each forward step as carefully as if both ankles hurt him.

It was the flare of a match up ahead, some moments later, that gave him his bearings and quickened his energies to meet the demand. Smoking under such circumstances was dangerously foolish, and the sentry's doing so telegraphed that he was bored and off guard. Twig spotted him after another moment of creeping silently forward. The man was using a boulder to keep himself from being seen from the trail coming out between the buttes. He had a hand braced on the rock and was looking the other way. He had left his horse in the brush behind the rock. It swung its head to look toward Twig but made no noise.

Twig had the man dead to rights before he called out in a voice magnified in the vast silence.

'Lift your hands and don't turn around or you're dead!'

The sentry jerked as if the words had been bullets cutting into his body. He had a hand gun, as well as a rifle that he had leaned against the rock. Twig limped on in and emptied the fellow's holster, then ordered him to step away from the rifle and turn. The man was Walt Trumbull, who had helped Dill take delivery of the feeders brought down from the Okanogan. Twig caught up the rifle with his free hand.

'Where'd you come from?' Trumbull gasped.

'All that concerns you,' Twig returned, 'is that I'm leavin' on your horse. Pull off your belt.'

Trumbull was furious, but he was also at his captor's mercy and needed no reminder. Twig bound him hand and foot with the man's belt and his own, giving him no chance to make a fight. He used Trumbull's bandanna for a gag, then without much pity dragged him into the bushes behind the boulder where the horse was. He shoved the rifle back into the saddle boot and looped Trumbull's gunbelt on the saddle horn before he swung up. He didn't need all that artillery, but he didn't intend to leave it where Trumbull, if he worked himself free, could get at it.

Looking down at the man on the ground, he said, 'Somebody'll find you. When they do, tell your bosses Link Sands had nothin' to do with this. I helped myself to a horse out of his pasture last night. You leave him alone.'

For two hours afterward he picked his way westward moving from cover to cover and never venturing into the open without a long study of the starlit range off to his right. This was essential but it made slow going, and it would be nip and tuck to get to where he could feel himself reasonably safe before daylight. And he had grown aware of another handicap, that one within himself.

He needed rest so badly that at times dizziness assailed him so that his empty stomach churned and he had to hold onto the saddle horn. His wrenched ankle had become a steady ache, and each step of the horse stirred up the soreness that had spread all over his battered body.

He took a chance on resting and was doing so, hidden in the shadows of some rocks, when he heard sound from the country behind him. The natural noises of the night seemed to part to let it through, and it was that of massed hooves drumming in the distance. He stared in that direction with dull eyes. They were too distant for him to see them in the night, but he knew they were coming toward him.

He had known when he dragged Trumbull into the brush that hiding him might buy little time. Anyone finding his post deserted would be instantly suspicious and could make a good enough guess at what had happened. Whoever had made this discovery had rousted enough men for a real pursuit. Twig settled this in his mind and considered his own move. He would have to go some to stay ahead of them. Even if he could do so, it was all too probable that there were other east-side men ahead of him to head him off. He hated to think of it, but his best chance was to cut back into the scablands, try to cross them, and then go on along the far side. The alarm might not have spread over there, and if it had he would be no worse off than now.

He started at once, heading south to where faint, starlighted shapes seemed to offer a chance to hide. It was more than that, for when he reached the place he found a dry wash running out from between broken cliffs. In the night he didn't have to worry about sign and he rode boldly along the bottom of the wash. For his own assurance, he stopped then and waited while the sound of the oncoming horses came nearer, grew loud, and then began to recede. Then he followed the wash on into the roughs.

He had luck again, for in seasons of heavy rains the wash drained a considerable part of the area. That gave him water courses to follow between rearing eminences or across small, open pockets, and he could still keep working south. But it cost him more time. And he hadn't moved a mile closer to the river in the several hours it took to cross and come out on the Rock Creek side.

Yet he felt encouraged. There seemed to be nothing ahead but empty country, so before he tackled it he stopped in the last rocks to rest himself and the horse. While he waited he ate one of the biscuits he had carried inside his shirt, drank from the canteen, and then decided to allow himself the luxury of a smoke. This was partly to keep him from falling asleep, for he knew that if he sat down or even closed his eyes standing up he would be gone. He feared this kind of drowsiness for if it gained too strong a grip he would surrender in indifference to his fate. Like a man freezing to death or a man so badly hurt that unconsciousness was a welcome relief.

When he swung back into the saddle he judged by the stars that he still had three or four hours of night. This decided him to keep edging the scabs as he had done on the other side and give himself a place to duck to if need be.

The new trouble developed so swiftly it was inescapable. He hadn't believed that anybody on this side would patrol so far west of the big coulee, at least so soon. But there the man was, riding over a crest in the rolling ground, hardly a hundred feet ahead and coming toward him. The fellow saw him in the same moment, and the shock of it seemed to paralyze both of them.

For Twig it was a double impact. The rider was Stringer Hames.

Hames let out a yell that carried all the hatred he had brought away from Ruby. It entered Twig like an electric shock, and then he was moving himself. He saw muzzle flare ahead of him. He heard the roar of a gun and felt the brain-jolting impact of a bullet even while he lifted his own pistol and fired.

His horse reared, and he collapsed onto its neck to stick in the saddle. The horse came down and wheeled, but he managed to saw it to a standstill.

Hames's horse had bolted and was clattering off to the east. Then Twig's staring eyes rested on the unmoving shape of Hames, there on the ground. He forced his jittery horse forward, ready for more trouble, but it grew evident that Hames wasn't feigning. Holstering his gun, Twig put a hand on the spreading numbness in his own left side. It was high, almost in the armpit and his fingers grew warm and wet. Then he realized that the hoofbeats he still heard weren't those of Hames's horse, for he could see that it had stopped. Somebody else had been near enough to hear the shots.

Twig had only to fling a glance at the roughs to know he couldn't enter them again in the shape he was in now. But he had absorbed too many blows in the past twenty-four hours to panic. This side would be swarming with danger very soon. By then the men on the far side would have had time to realize they had lost their quarry. The only thing left to them would be to send men ahead to cut him off at the river. They were as well acquainted as he was with the few places it could be crossed in high water. They would watch Sands's place, too, and the direct route southwest to Wenatchee City.

But there was something they might not think of. Either Abner or Zeke could bring his boat to the bank at quite a number of places and would do so if it was flagged. That gave him several choices. And the only way his enemies could catch on would be by accidentally cutting, or painstakingly following, his tracks. He rode quietly over the crest and on the far decline lifted his horse to a gallop. When, ten minutes later, he reined down to listen there was no sound of pursuit. Hames's body had stopped the man or men who had been with him for the time being.

That was small comfort, for his wound was bleeding profusely. At the end of an hour he was succumbing to a torpor too powerful to be held off. He fought it stubbornly, yet he lost track of time and distance and almost of direction. The horse had slowed to a lazy walk, but he didn't try to hurry it again. He grew very thirsty and more and more often drank from the canteen.

All at once it was daylight, and Twig realized he had been asleep or had passed out. He started to take another drink only to find that he had emptied the canteen. He tossed it away and tried to bring his blurred eyes into focus so he could figure out where he was. Nothing seemed familiar, or even distinct, anywhere he looked. It didn't much matter. He only wanted to rest. Nothing could be as alluring as the thought of sleep, not even Lorna's ripe lips. Lorna? She had disowned him, the same as Oak had. And he didn't care a fig for she wasn't worth the little finger of Melissa Brown. Melissa. There was a girl who measured a man by what he had inside of him rather than out...

In another moment of clarity he realized that the sun had climbed much higher and was no longer behind him where it should have been. He pondered this and realized what had happened. Unguided, the horse had begun to meander and finally had taken it into its head to go home. The land wheeled away in rolling emptiness all around, and there was only the sun to tell him that for perhaps two hours he had been moving toward Injun Creek. The jolt of this was enough to sweep the vapors out of his head for a while.

He reined in and took a look all about. Nobody was in sight, nor could he see a dust. He could have ridden right into somebody's arms without knowing it, yet somehow had avoided that. His wound seemed to have stopped bleeding, but his shirt was caked and stiff. The affected arm felt numb and strange, yet he could move it so the bones seemed to be all right. His ankle hurt even worse than his side and had swollen until the boot felt like a wrapping of rubber bands.

Drowsiness welled up in him again, but he fought it for he had to stay alert to guide the horse and stay aboard because if he fell off he would stay where he landed. He made a determined effort to concentrate. The sun by then was halfway up the sky. If he put it behind him and kept it there, he ought to strike the river somewhere along the long S-curve between the Chelan and Entiat. If he got there too late to flag the upboat, he could try for the one coming down. Two nights had passed now since he got off the *Chief,* so Zeke would be going up that day and Abner coming down.

And Melissa would be in Wenatchee City, which he had to reach. He remembered how cool and pleasant it had been, sitting with her in the evening on the deck outside her door...

He had no sense of having covered much ground, but all at once he realized that the horse was trotting. He knew it smelled water, which had guided and hurried it, and the only water in that whole God-forsaken country was in the river. He smiled, thinking how he would soak his hot, aching body when they got there. He would find something for a pole, use his shirt for a flag, then lie in the cold, clean water.

Then they were at the river at a place where it would have taken a horse with a twenty-foot neck to get a drink. Twig stared down at the wide, swollen, rushing water that came from the snows as far away as the Rockies. He had to move upstream or down even to find a place where a steamboat could put in to shore. But all the will he owned seemed to have been focused on getting there. It was used up completely, and he felt himself slipping and falling from the saddle into the black cushion of unconsciousness.

CHAPTER EIGHTEEN

Dill looked down at the dead man and knew that in spite of his utmost efforts everything had gone to pieces yet again. Even Lublin was sobered, although he tried to be jocular as usual.

'Well,' Lublin drawled. 'Stringer got his second chance and his second slug. Right through the brisket.'

Dill growled like a cornered animal, which was what he had begun to feel like. They knew for sure now that their quarry was Twig, who had a way of popping up where least expected and not showing at all where he was expected. Dill remembered with bitterness his few moments of elation, the night before, when they heard the four rifle shots over toward Rock Creek and went boiling out of the cirque to investigate. It had been to find an excited sentry sure he had spotted Twig and maybe hit him. They had beat the brush and rocks for an hour before they found the wounded coyote whose noise had touched off the shooting.

They had gone back to the cirque and had been there hardly another hour when a man from the Injun Creek side fogged in to say

Walt Trumbull had deserted his post or been forced to leave it. So everyone had rushed over to that side, and they finally found Trumbull tied up in the brush and learned what had happened to him. Lublin had sent a party smoking down that side with orders to head for the river crossings if they didn't scare anything up. With Twig on a good horse, finally, he could cover ground fast.

The final blow had come from yet another rider who reported that Twig was not only back on the Rock Creek side but had killed Stringer Hames. There had been no one left in the cirque then but himself and Lublin. Lublin had sent the man on to tell the Rock Creek crew to head for the river, too. Then Dill and he had come down here where Stringer Hames had squared off against his last man, arriving just as daylight did.

Lublin had been poking around examining the ground. Suddenly he called, 'Stringer might have got in a lick himself, this time.' Dill went over to see a few dark stains on the ground at Lublin's feet. 'Blood, sure as hell,' Lublin added. 'Twig's or the horse's. Either one would slow him down and maybe bring him to a stop.'

Dill was ready to grab at any small straw of hope. 'Come on,' he said, not needing Lublin's help to know what they had to do. 'If he plays out short of the river, we've got to find him before some outsider does.'

For many hours he had lived with the knowledge of what must happen to Twig if they could make it happen. Murder was still a chilling thought to him, but if it was all that would save him he was ready for it. He had no idea how it could be accounted for afterward, but he was improvising in desperation now, shorn of the cool wiliness that had worked for him so long so well.

Neither of them gave another thought to Hames, leaving him to stare up with empty eyes at the morning sky. They saw how Twig had eased his way over the crest, then lifted the speed of his horse. So it wasn't the horse that had been hit, although all along the way there were more of those dark, dribbled spots.

'He's bleedin' like a stuck hog,' Lublin commented. 'At that rate he won't last.'

Even so, Twig had ridden hard for quite a distance, making west for the river as expected. Then the track pattern changed, showing that the horse had slowed to a trot and finally to a walk. Dill and Lublin rode faster than that, for the sign was easy to follow. Yet Dill wasn't comforted by the thought of soon overtaking Twig and catching him alive. From Trumbull's account, Twig had two six-shooters and a rifle, and he had demonstrated an unusual marksmanship.

The sun mounted and grew hotter, and

presently they found the empty saddle canteen beside the trail. This encouraged Dill. A wounded man was a fevered man, and fever robbed the brain of its sharpness. The horse they followed was only poking along by then. Finally the sign showed that it had stopped, tromped around aimlessly a bit, and then had started off to the northeast.

'What do you make of that?' Dill said. 'He try to double back?'

Lublin pushed back his hat and wiped sweat off his forehead. 'Looks like he headed for Injun Creek, but I'm damned if I'd know why.'

Just the same Twig had ridden steadily toward Injun Creek on an unhurried horse. The trackers followed, puzzled but compelled to stay with it. They had covered a couple of miles before they reached a place where the horse had stopped and again changed direction.

'Must've seen some of our boys,' Lublin decided, 'and tried to shy around 'em. I sure don't like the way he's holdin' up.'

Dill liked it no better, for time and again they seemed to have Twig under their thumb only to have him slip away. Unwillingly but inevitably he was seeing the man whose existence had been denied for years to Oak and even to himself. The kid was a tough rooster, and he had grit and wit.

The horse tracks now pointed northwest, which was as bewildering as the other change of direction. There was no place in that whole reach of the river where it could be forded or even swum during high water. 'Maybe I got it figured out,' Lublin commented. 'He's out of his head, and the cayuse is boss. Otherwise he'd know that ridin' into them river bends is a sure way to get trapped.'

It was hardly ten minutes after that when they reined in, both of them staring northward. There was a dust over there almost abreast of them but at quite a distance. Dill lifted his field glasses from their case and put them to his eyes. The moment he had the lenses in focus he knew things were breaking his way at last.

'What is it?' Lublin asked.

'Horse,' Dill said in rising triumph. 'The one he took off of Walt. Reins on its neck. Empty saddle.'

'He's been dumped,' Lublin said gleefully. 'Come on. Let's catch the critter.'

That was Dill's desire, too, and they forgot the sign and headed north. The third horse kept going, sticking to a northeast course. Dill knew that as soon as it had lost its rider it had started home to Injun Creek. And somewhere in this lonely country the man who could destroy him lay helpless and, because of the tracks, a cinch to find.

When it grew aware of them, the other horse broke into a trot. But they came in on it easily, rode with it a short distance, and when they stopped it stopped, too. Swinging down, they went over to it, and Lublin caught its reins.

'Look at that,' Dill said happily. The saddle was slippery with blood and the saddle blanket on that side was soaked.

'He's finished,' Lublin agreed. 'A man hurt too bad to stick his saddle sure couldn't get out of this country on foot.'

There was something even more comforting. Trumbull's pistol rig was still hung on the saddle horn, and the rifle was still in the boot. That made it certain that Twig's quitting the saddle hadn't been voluntary. If he had decided to fort up somewhere, unable to ride any longer, he would have wanted all the firearms he could get.

'Well, let's find some shade and take a breather,' Lublin said. 'There's no rush now. He ain't goin' anywhere, even if he ain't already dead.'

Dill hoped he would be dead. And while he was anxious to find out he dreaded it, too, so he was agreeable to Lublin's suggestion that they rest. Both of them had been going it over twenty-four hours without letup and without much food. Leading the Injun Creek horse, they made their way back along its trail. Presently when they sighted a flattop off to the south, they rode over into its shade and stopped.

There was a sudden serenity on the range, a look of golden promise. With Twig gone forever, nothing could stand between this wheeling grazing land and all the rest that OT claimed and the man who had earned his right to it times over. Yet something still cast a shadow on this pleasing vista, Dill remembered – Lublin, who had seated himself on a shaded rock and started to roll a cigarette. Dill stood looking at him with thoughtful eyes.

Lublin licked the cigarette paper, then expressed his high good humor with a laugh.

'You know how we're gonna put this over with Oak Tully and the law?' he asked. He meant to say, not ask. 'We're gonna tell the gospel truth. It was Twig that killed Stringer and Stringer that got Twig. They were personal enemies. Must be friends of Twig he told about Stringer tryin' to dry-gulch him at Ruby. And that's all there was to it.'

'How about the stuff in the coulee?' Dill asked.

'We're the only ones who know it's there. When the excitement over the killings dies down, we'll move it to my Idaho spread, nice and easy.'

'Oh no. Not this bunch, and not the other bunches you'd force out of me later.'

Lublin raised his eyes from the match with

which he had lighted his cigarette. It was to look straight into the barrel of the gun in Dill's hand.

'Hey.' Lublin's voice was flat and all gone. 'What's this?'

Dill only looked at him with merciless eyes.

'Come, now,' Lublin said anxiously. 'You ain't gonna get this far in the clear and then go loco. Put that gun back in the leather.'

'You lost the one friend who might have taken it up for you,' Dill said. 'With both of you gone, the others'll run like scared hens. And that yarn you were gonna tell didn't go far enough. You want to hear the rest?'

'Come on,' Lublin wheedled. 'Put away that gun.'

Dill wanted to make him sit there, sweating and listening to why he wasn't the only one with brains. 'I've had the same suspicions Twig did,' he went on. 'That you and your cronies have been rustlin' OT poor. I've been tryin' to catch you at it, myself. Twig beat me to it, that's all, and run into Stringer. They shot it out, all right. I got there too late to help, but I killed you in a kill or be killed showdown about it. How does that listen to you, Sid?'

Lublin's face was drained and pale. 'It won't work,' he said weakly. 'Your name's on all them bills of sale.'

'Forged. Every damned one.'

242

'The tally books–'

'Doctored before they were ever turned over to me.'

Lublin accepted it at last, knew he had to fight for his life. Dill saw his muscles bunching and shot – once, twice, and then again.

The jarred air seemed to crack in his ears for moments afterward. Then he lifted his eyes from the bleeding figure on the ground and swung them from horizon to horizon. There still was no one in all that lonely country but himself and a dead man and another who was dead or would be soon.

The feeling of high well-being had left him. Yet he was without remorse for what he had done and cool enough to roll and smoke a cigarette. The horses had shied off, but none of them had run away. He walked over to the one Twig had taken off Trumbull, put the reins back on its neck, gave it a whack with his hat and sent it on its way again to Injun Creek. He left Lublin's horse there with what remained of Lublin, mounted his own, and rode south to where they had first picked up the riderless horse.

Moments later he was following the tracks the horse had made coming out of some place deep in the river bend. It was almost noon by then, but Dill was oblivious of the mounting heat and his own weariness. It was all but over. As soon as he had made sure of Twig he would head for Wenatchee

City to make the report he had outlined to Lublin. Thanks to Hames's effort to kill Twig at Ruby, it would go over. Lublin's death only rounded that out and made the whole thing make sense.

And now Twig. The only explanation for his heading into this section was the one Lublin had offered. Twig was out of his head or sufficiently so he didn't realize he was riding into a cul-de-sac. Dill felt confident of finding him helpless, if not dead. Yet once he had sighted the river, far ahead of him, he rode with care. Then he came to the river to find nothing but mute testimony of what must have happened there. This not only bewildered Dill, it put the touch of cold fear back in his heart.

Bloody earth showed that Twig had fallen from the horse, as supposed, and had laid there unstirring for a long while. But boot prints disclosed that he had recovered sufficiently to get to his feet again. This would have been to find the horse gone and that it was impossible to cross the river at that place with or without a horse. And then Twig had moved on. The ground was so rocky Dill had to hunt around to find which way he had gone. It proved to be upstream into equally deserted country, suggesting again that he didn't know what he was doing.

Again confident that his enemy could not escape, Dill swung onto his horse and rode slowly along the river shore. The banks stayed high above the water. Now and then there was an earthy stretch on top to show that Twig had not only staggered, he was dragging a leg, or at least favoring a foot. This kept Dill moving slowly and with extreme care, for at any moment he might overtake him.

And then, ahead, he saw that the bank at last broke down to the water. This was a spot he had never seen before, and what puzzled him was something slapping from some kind of pole, stirred by the river breeze. The area was open, and there wasn't a soul in sight, yet he came down to this disturbed by a sense of something awful about to go wrong. There wasn't a tree or even a patch of brush anywhere near, and yet that pole—

All at once Dill dropped caution and rode on down to prove to himself that what he feared couldn't be. Yet the flapping thing tied to the pole was a shirt, torn and bloody. There were old horse tracks all around, and he knew how there happened to be a pole at that lonely place. It had been brought there sometime in the past and set up by some settler in the vicinity to make a landing for the steamboats.

Twig had known about this. He had headed for it to escape the men sent to guard the river crossings. He had made it and – Dill shook his head dazedly. It couldn't be, yet it had happened, for Twig was gone and he couldn't have swum the river even if he had been in prime condition. He had flagged one of the boats. By now he was on his way out to complete the ruin of everything.

Dill's next thought was of Lublin's body. The man he had murdered in the only murder of his life. How was that to be accounted for now, when there were men who knew he was the last to be with Lublin? When a good tracker could prove the two of them had ridden side by side from the far-off coulee to where Lublin's body would be found? Then he thought beyond that to the OT brooders back in the coulee and the futility of even trying to scatter them. Nothing now could stave off an audit. An audit that would lead to a hanging rope, instead of the loss of his job and perhaps a few years in the pen.

Yet he had to play out his string. Swinging his horse about, he headed for Wenatchee City to make his last desperate play, this time not for a ranch and a woman but for his very life.

CHAPTER NINETEEN

Twig wasn't sure whether he had hard rock under his sore, throbbing body, or the quivering support of a moving steamboat, or a real soft bed. The first two were mixed together in his wakening thoughts, yet his head seemed to be on a pillow. He didn't seem to have on many clothes, so that patches of bare skin touched what had the feel of bed sheets. He had tried to open his eyes, but they were too hot and aching. Anyway, his mind was too tired and woozy to pick at any new problems just then.

So he lay thinking about the apparent fact that, in spite of all those problems, he wasn't dead. He had felt inescapably close to it when he came to, there on the bank of the river, to discover that he had finally fallen off his horse and that it had got away. Yet he had found strength enough to get on his feet. And his head had cleared enough to let him get his bearings.

He had realized that he wasn't far down from Amherst's Landing, which could be made by the steamers even at high-water stages. So he had started, walking on a foot that seemed like a club appended to his leg

247

instead of a part of himself, causing him to stumble, fall, get up and fall again. But he had made the landing and hung his shirt on the pole there before, once more, he passed out.

The next thing he could remember was being aboard the *Arrow*. He hadn't been clearheaded enough to figure it out previously, but the upboat had come by the lonely landing not long after he got there himself. It had put in, found and taken him aboard, and, seeing the shape he was in, Zeke had put about and headed downstream full steam to get him to a doctor. So he was in Wenatchee City now, but not in a bunk on a boat, for they were nowhere near as soft as this bed.

And then Twig opened his eyes to see Melissa smiling down on him as if he had just got back from an absence of ten years.

'About time you woke up,' she said and blinked back what surely looked like tears. 'I've never seen such a lay abed.'

'Hello, Melissa,' he said weakly. 'It your bed?'

'Well, for heaven's sake, not at present.'

'We're gonna take care of that,' he mumbled. 'Real soon.'

'Are we, Twig?'

'If you're willin'.'

'Willing?' Those sure enough were tears in her eyes. She bit her lip and said, 'But we better talk about that later. Your father's here.'

'Oak?'

Twig tried to sit up but fell back groaning. He turned his head. While he didn't know how Oak had managed to get there, there he was, sitting in his wheelchair. He looked back at Melissa, who should have had rainbows in her eyes they were so full of sunshine and moisture. What was it he'd thought once about her having no frailty and tenderness and promise of sweet surrender? She turned to leave the room, but Oak spoke gently.

'Stay. You got more right to be here than I have.'

'Howdy, Oak,' Twig said and managed to grin. 'Looks like we're a couple of sorefoots. Did you bring your cribbage board?'

'That's for later, too,' Oak said and returned the grin. 'You've got more'n a game leg. Doc says you were down to your last drop of blood. Which was enough, for it was the right blood.'

'It sure was,' Melissa agreed.

Twig understood why she kept nibbling her lip and twitching her nose and batting her eyes. He managed to say, 'It sounds like you figured things out.'

Oak's face darkened. 'Zeke told me part of it. Dill the rest. Not that he realized he was doin' it.'

249

'You've seen Dill?'

'Last night,' Oak said. 'He come foggin' in to tell me how you two were workin' for the same end all along without either of you realizin' it. How he got into such a hassle with 'em himself that he had to kill Lublin. Seems there was forgery and crooked countin' and rustlin' over there for years.'

'And you believed that?' Twig gasped.

'Not for a minute. How could I, when he lied to me about you from the time you were a tadpole.'

Twig felt dizzy, but not because of his physical condition. 'How did you finally get that through your head?'

'You couldn't have been the washout he made you seem and stood up to me and done what you did. It was more'n Dill could do, and that's what turned the trick with me.'

'Where is he?'

'Bein' held for the sheriff. I guess you don't know that Lorna promised herself to him. Now she's lamentin' the fearful way she done you wrong. She says it was only because she was provoked with you for lettin' me down.'

'You don't seem to put much stock in that, either.'

Oak shook his head. 'I've got reason to be sensitive about women who'll give themselves to the man they think has the best prospects. It's what her mother done to me. I'll take care of her moneywise, but I reckon she can find some other town to live in.'

Twig felt his throat tighten up the way his ankle had in the boot. To cover it, he said, 'How did you manage to get down here?'

'Found I can travel better than I knew. When I heard they'd brought you in, I started rollin'. And I made it here.' Oak grinned. 'That was yesterday. Melissa was good enough to let me stay.'

Twig knew what that meant. He had the only bed in her cramped quarters, so Melissa and Oak had set their vigil together, drawing them closer together than Oak could ever have felt with Lorna, whose devotion had been guileful. He turned his eyes to Melissa and he liked the way she was looking at him. He knew it would be this way whether he went back to OT, stayed on the river, or decided to quit both and raise hogs. He knew it would stay this way with Oak, too, no matter what he did, for they finally knew each other.

Somehow the problem of what he would do had got settled, too. He would return to OT but to shape it to its times the way Oak had shaped it in his day. With the two families united, maybe Oak would get interested in transportation and see it as a new and useful way to expand. To meet the changing times. To keep the Tully name a big one in the Wenatchee country. It was something he and Oak would talk about, he decided. Over a cribbage board. Later.

The publishers hope that this book has given you enjoyable reading. Large Print Books are especially designed to be as easy to see and hold as possible. If you wish a complete list of our books please ask at your local library or write directly to:

The Golden West Large Print Books
Magna House, Long Preston,
Skipton, North Yorkshire.
BD23 4ND

This Large Print Book, for people
who cannot read normal print,
is published under the auspices of

THE ULVERSCROFT FOUNDATION

... we hope you have enjoyed this book.
Please think for a moment about those
who have worse eyesight than you ...
and are unable to even read or enjoy
Large Print without great difficulty.

You can help them by sending a
donation, large or small, to:

**The Ulverscroft Foundation,
1, The Green, Bradgate Road,
Anstey, Leicestershire, LE7 7FU,
England.**
or request a copy of our brochure for
more details.

The Foundation will use all donations
to assist those people who are visually
impaired and need special attention
with medical research, diagnosis
and treatment.

Thank you very much for your help.